Family Affairs

BOOKS BY THE AUTHOR

FAMILY AFFAIRS
THE CLANG BIRDS
TIGHT WHITE COLLAR
NO PLACE FOR HIDING
ONE EYE AND A MEASURING ROD
PICNIC IN BABYLON: A PRIEST'S JOURNAL
RUBRICS FOR A REVOLUTION
QUICK AS DANDELIONS

Family

Affairs

———◆———

John L'Heureux

DOUBLEDAY & COMPANY, INC., GARDEN CITY, NEW YORK, 1974

Grateful acknowledgment is made to the magazines in which some of these stories first appeared:

SOMETHING MISSING and A FAMILY AFFAIR, *The Atlantic Monthly*; THE PLUMBER, *Four Quarters*, Copyright © 1971 by La Salle College; FOX AND SWAN, *Transatlantic Review*, Copyright © 1971 by Joseph F. McCrindle; THE INNOCENTS, *The Boston Review of the Arts*; STILL MORE ON THE NOSE, *Works in Progress*, Number 3.

Library of Congress Cataloging in Publication Data

L'Heureux, John.
    Family affairs.

    CONTENTS: Something missing.—Completed work.—The plumber. [etc.]
    I. Title.
PZ4.L685Fam [PS3562.H4] 813'.5'4
ISBN 0-385-03671-X
Library of Congress Catalog Card Number 73-18777

For
Jeanne and John Rush

CONTENTS

I

SOMETHING MISSING   3

COMPLETED WORK   17

THE PLUMBER   29

BENJAMIN   43

A FAMILY AFFAIR   65

II

FOX AND SWAN   99

THE INNOCENTS   113

SINS OF THOUGHT, SINS OF DESIRE   129

STILL MORE ON THE NOSE   143

A FEW NECESSARY QUESTIONS   169

Family Affairs

Part One

SOMETHING MISSING

AFTER THE fire in the school, reporters tried to find out all they could about the Goldfarbs. Information about the son, Isaac, was repeatedly self-contradictory, and about Avram they learned nothing at all. He had come either from Hungary or Holland and was currently employed by a music publishing firm. That was all anybody knew. They were a quiet suburban family like any other. There was no story in them.

Avram Goldfarb was a child prodigy of seven, a pianist, when a drunken Nazi broke his hands. The soldier had been sent to round up the whole family, but the boy played Schubert so beautifully that he took only the father and mother and left the boy behind, having first taken care to smash his small hands with a rifle butt. At nine Avram had murdered a man who had threatened to reveal his hiding place, and at ten he escaped to Holland where he grew up, married a German girl, and taught music. He was determined his son would be the pianist he himself could have been; when his wife became pregnant, therefore, they emigrated to America where, everyone knew, opportunities abound. Thus Isaac Joseph Goldfarb was born in Bridgeport, Connecticut.

Isaac was a child of extraordinary beauty. His large luminous eyes seemed always filled with tears, and his hair was a mass of glossy black curls. "What a beautiful baby! What is her name?" women would sometimes ask, and Karen Goldfarb would smile with pleasure. She had wanted a daughter. When he was three, he hacked a path down the center of his hair with his mother's scissors because the boy next door had called him a girl. After that Karen took him regularly to the barber shop.

As he grew, Isaac displayed a keen intelligence and great depths of emotion. Not only did he throw tantrums, he knew when not to throw them; he could delay his fury for hours until the time was right. "Temperament in an artist is good," his father said, and at once set him to the piano. Isaac's hands were long and white, with an impressive open spread, and in very short time they flowed across the keys with a life and control of their own. The boy's technical mastery was amazingly in advance of his years or his training, and his father held great hopes for him. With time the boy's technique became nearly flawless. Still, the father said, something was missing. Had he been more honest, he would have admitted that the missing something was genius; but his life depended on that not being so, and he spent much of his day trying to infuse his own genius into his angry, despairing son. Neither understood who the other was.

Isaac was persecuted by the other children at school. At first they hated him because he was beautiful and was cooed at and tickled by the teachers. Later they hated him because he was unlike them; he wore short pants and knee stockings; while they played baseball, he practiced piano; he seemed to think he was somehow better than they. He was a sissy. Finally they hated him out of habit. He didn't belong. They knew it and he knew it. Before he was twelve, he had been condemned forever.

And so it came as a relief to Isaac when, after that first disastrous year at high school, his father moved the family from Bridgeport to a small town outside Boston where he had been offered a job with a music publishing firm.

That summer was the happiest time of Isaac's life. Everything was beginning new. His father, busy with his new job, did not have time to hound him about his practice, about the something missing. His mother had given up hoping for a daughter and had stopped thinking of Isaac as a substitute. He was alone, and he spent long hours walking in the woods, sketching the pine trees by the reservoir, imagining a future in which there would be nothing to fear. The less he practiced piano, the more his sketching improved. He began to think he might give up music for painting. And then he discovered his voice. It was a thin, sweet sound that seemed to come from somewhere outside of him; a tone not of complaint but of intense sorrow, the legacy of thousands of years of exile. All that summer he sang in the woods, convinced that in the fall everything would be different.

But in late August his face began to break out. By the time school began in September, his face and neck swarmed with ripe pustules, three and four running into one another to form a sickening purple mass between his nose and his lip. Karen could not bear to look at him, her beautiful son, disgusting. Avram scarcely noticed, aware as he was only of the boy's absence of soul, his brilliant articulating fingers on the keyboard telling always of something missing.

The first day of school was everything Isaac had feared. He had succeeded in registering as Joseph Goldfarb and had been careful not to speak unless spoken to, not to walk in that way people always made fun of, not to gesture with his beautiful hands. Despite his face, he would succeed as a man. In fact, his face might be a help; no one would notice now the long curled lashes or the limpid eyes. They nudged one another whenever he spoke, but that might be only because he was new and they had all been together for a long time. And at lunch he walked alone behind animated groups of three and four, but after all he was new and must give the others a chance to get used to him. Yes. It was because he was new. He wouldn't force himself on anyone this time, wouldn't drive them away with his . . . whatever it was. He would eventually have friends and be like the rest of them. No one knew him here.

After lunch Isaac reported to the locker room for physical education class. He had trouble finding 2-A, not realizing that 2-A was a euphemism for the cellar, and so he came late.

The locker room was a cavernous cement affair that reeked of disinfectant. Jutting from the wall were six long benches, and built above the benches were racks for clothes and equipment. To the left was a wire cage filled with baskets, each marked with the owner's number, containing sneakers, socks, supporters, shorts, and whatever more elaborate equipment the boy might have— knee pads or ankle stiffeners or straps for eyeglasses. There was a window in the cage, and the coach, a short beefy man whose huge chest and stomach muscles had long since gone to fat, stood behind it handing out the baskets to their owners. To the right was a short flight of stairs leading to another cement room, this one smaller, equipped only with spigots on one wall and a huge rubber tray of disinfectant on the other.

Entering the locker room, Isaac stood dumfounded. Most of the boys had on gym shorts by this time and were noisily comparing biceps or punching one another or pretending to. A few stood there naked, putting on athletic socks or supporters. Never having seen anyone naked before, he could not believe they all stripped bare this way in front of one another. He blushed and looked around him, frightened.

"Hey, you!" Buck Carey, the coach, stood behind the wire grill. "You're supposed to be on time, you know. You ever hear of being on time?"

The noisy chatter fell off.

"I'm sorry. I didn't know where . . ." Isaac could hear his voice and knew it was too high. He stopped. The coach, studying him in evident disgust, said nothing. "I'm sorry. What do I do?" He hoped he would be sent away.

"What do you do?" He looked around and addressed the boys. "He wants to know what he does." They laughed as they were expected to. "You strip. First you strip."

Painfully Isaac began to remove his clothes. The blood had rushed to his head, and he was so dizzy he thought he would fall over. No one said anything; he knew everyone was looking at him. Finally he stood before them naked.

"Now what?" the coach asked him.

"Now what?" Isaac repeated.

"Now you put on your jock and your shorts. Unless you want to go out on the field like that." Everyone laughed.

"I don't have any. I didn't know."

"What are you? A freshman or something?"

"I . . . no . . . I'm new. I'm a sophomore, but this is my first year. At this school, I mean." If only he could cover himself, but that would be worse. They'd make comments.

"Next time bring your equipment. Today you can use common stock. Understand?"

"Yes, sir."

"Yes, Coach," he corrected.

"Yes, Coach."

"All right now. Name?" He scanned the class list; he knew every name but one.

"Joseph Goldfarb. Joe." He swallowed. He glanced around for reassurance, but the boys avoided his eyes.

"Nope. There's no Joseph Goldfarb here. There's an Isaac Goldfarb. You sure you're not Isaac?"

"Well, Isaac is my middle name. The name I go by is . . ."

Ed LaCroix, quarterback and captain of the football team, made a show of looking at Isaac's privates and announced loudly, "Yeah, he's Isaac all right, Coach."

Isaac's explanation was lost in the tense, uproarious laughter. Dimly he understood what Ed LaCroix knew well from association with the coach: only Isaac's humiliation would stop his badgering. It had to end that way. It always did.

Before school let out everyone knew the hilarious story about the new boy's encounter with Buck Carey.

Two weeks passed during which Isaac was ignored altogether. He had thought this was what he wanted, but he found isolation more suffocating than insult; it was as if they were telling him he didn't exist. His skin became worse, glossy red bumps puffing up his lips and blotting his forehead, until at last the terror of facing school each day kept him constantly on the brink of tears.

Avram Goldfarb, ignoring the threat of tears, went on urging the boy to deepen his playing. "You have no soul," he would scream, "look at me, look at me; you have no soul." And shaking him violently by the shoulders, he would stare deep into the boy's eyes where he saw nothing, nothing at all. He did not guess and would not have understood his son's terror of school. Karen suspected but said nothing; she was disappointed in her son, who was not manly and authoritative like his father. In school Isaac would sketch caricatures of his teachers and his fellow students, but usually of himself—his hooked nose and his long, skinny body easily lending themselves to caricature—and at home he would walk in the woods singing in his pure, sad voice. He was totally alone.

There were two people who had some inkling of what went on in Isaac's mind: Buck Carey, who felt an unreasoning hatred whenever he saw the boy; and Ed LaCroix, who felt guilty for what he had done. Both quietly resolved to do something about their feelings. It was Miss Connolly who gave them their opportunity.

Despite the locker room story, or perhaps because of it, the teachers continued to call the boy Joseph. They never knew what to make of him. He turned away from the few kindnesses offered him, and yet he seemed so lonely. And certainly there was no denying that he was terrible to look at, Miss Connolly thought. He was bright and sensitive. Somebody should help him. His essays, grammatically sound and well-structured, were always the best in the class; they had what all the others lacked, a completely unfettered imagination, perhaps too unfettered, and it was on the pretext of talking about this—his imagination—that she kept him after school. Their conversation, halting and stumbling as it was, uncovered to Miss Connolly a depth of suffering and violence that frightened her. Nonetheless she carried through with her original intention and told Isaac, before dismissing him, that perhaps he found his facial condition embarrassing and perhaps he could see a skin doctor. She felt it might help, she said, smiling with genuine kindness. Tears leaped to his eyes; it was a long time since anyone had smiled that way at him. When he left, Miss Connolly reported to Mr. Gorham, the student counselor, that she was worried about the boy. Mr. Gorham promised he would look into it, but busy as he was with four hundred student profiles, each to be made out in triplicate, he did not get around to Isaac until it was too late.

Two more weeks passed, and Isaac stole the money from his mother and went to a skin doctor, who gave him a bottle of pink fluid which, when dry, covered his face with an opaque film. He used this each night, and then one day worked up courage enough to wear it to school. It caused a sensation.

"Joe Goldfarb is wearing makeup!"

"Josie, you mean."

"Ike the kike forgot his lipstick."

In the girls' room nobody talked of anything else, and in the boys' room each tried to make his comment on Isaac the funniest and the most obscene. Buck Carey—since there was no phys ed that day—had to wait until football practice to share his remarks with the boys he knew he could trust.

Isaac's makeup was the talk of the school, and so he was not surprised at the end of the day to discover on the main bulletin board one of his own caricatures of himself; someone had drawn a skirt on it. He was surprised, however, when Ed LaCroix pushed through the giggling crowd and without a word tore the picture down. The next day Ed's steady girl, a sophomore, smiled at Isaac and did not turn away.

Linda Davis had smiled at him and meant it. All during the day Isaac turned this over in his mind. Perhaps it was still possible. Perhaps he could still have friends and be like all the others. Perhaps. Please, God, yes, he found himself saying, though he did not believe in God and had never prayed. Please, yes.

When phys ed period came, he skipped it. Filled with excitement at the possibility of a new life, he could not face the hard eyes and ugly tongue of Buck Carey, and so when the bell rang he slipped down the side stairs to the glee club room. It was another cement cavern, rendered nearly soundproof by the boiler that stood between it and the locker room. Nobody ever came here except the glee club and the band, so Isaac knew he would be safe. He sang to himself for a while, thinking of Linda, and then he played a Schubert sonata, but softly, very softly.

Buck Carey, having saved choice comments for Isaac, was not pleased to find he was absent.

"You, LaCroix," he said. "Go check the office and see if your friend has been excused. And then check study hall and the auditorium, see. And bring him back here in ten minutes." He had heard about LaCroix taking down the picture.

Ed LaCroix shifted his weight from foot to foot. "My friend?"

There was an unspoken understanding between them regarding how much liberty one could take with the other. Ed after all was a very good quarterback.

"Goldfarb, I mean. Go check the office, would you?" His tone was different now.

"Yes, I'll go."

He took a shortcut through the boiler room and, passing the glee club door, he thought he heard music. He pushed open the peephole as Isaac began the sonata. Ed LaCroix, pleased for some reason he himself did not understand, listened for five minutes and then returned to the locker room.

"He's been excused. He hurt his foot or something."

"Foot. *My* foot. I'll get that fairy yet."

The next morning Isaac found on his desk a note telling him to report to the principal's office. Mr. Millar studied him for a moment as if he were something under a microscope—he had heard unpleasant reports about this difficult, high-strung young man— and then coldly summarized. "Coach Carey will see you after school in the locker room. If you are not there, Mr. Goldfarb, you will be suspended from this school. Is that clear?" And he dismissed him.

When he returned to his desk he did not notice Linda's smile. A feeling of doom hung over him all during the morning, and at lunch period, unable to eat anything, he walked by the river, letting his eye follow the curve of branches where they bent to the water, pretending to himself that the other world of cruelty did not exist.

"I'll survive him," he told himself. "I'll survive them all."

The afternoon was clear and windy, with just enough nip in the air to be perfect football weather. Buck Carey sent his team, jogging in their bulky uniforms, out to the field for calisthenics while he lingered behind with Isaac. The boy's pimpled face disgusted him.

"Okay, Ikey. You decided to show up today, did you? Huh? Decide to show up?"

Isaac stared at the cement floor. Three hours from now all this will be over, he thought.

"I'm talking to you!" He grabbed the boy's skinny shoulder and pressed his thumb painfully into the joint. "Nothing to say, huh? Nothing to say to the coach?" He brought his face close to Isaac's, and his voice was intense. "Well, listen to me, boy. I'm gonna run your ass right off. Now get out on that field."

Isaac joined the uniformed football team. No one acknowledged him, and he was grateful for that; humiliation became some-how easier as it became less personal. He felt now almost like an anonymous viewer at his own execution.

And then Ed LaCroix approached him.

"Listen, you want a ride home afterward? I'll give you a ride home. I'm going to meet Linda in 24, so if you get out first, go to 24. And don't let Carey get you down."

Before Isaac could even acknowledge his offer, Ed LaCroix dis-appeared into the crowd of milling athletes.

"Okay, men. Everybody in position. Come on. Come on. You, Goldfart, I want you in the front row over on the side." The coach seemed in good humor this afternoon. "We're only going coed for this afternoon, men, so don't get worried."

He paused for the ripple of laughter that came, though begrudg-ingly.

"Okay then, let's go, let's go. Jog in place, ONE two, ONE two, IN place, IN place. ONE two. Keep up with them, Goldfart."

For over an hour he barked commands, his attention so fixed on Isaac's situps and pushups and deep knee bends that he was oblivious to his bored and tired team. He was astonished that the skinny, sickly-looking boy did not collapse. He began to hope he wouldn't. Suddenly he saw himself as something more than a high school football coach; he was a savior. The little kike actually had guts enough to survive a calisthenics workout with some very tough guys. With a strong hand to guide him and toughen him up, he might yet become a man. A Buck Carey creation. Buck, married eight years, had no children of his own.

"Practice time! LaCroix, you take them through the offensive plays. Okay men, two teams. Break it up. And don't go easy on anybody, Ed."

The team broke and reassembled in two huddles as Buck Carey ambled over to Isaac, who was bent in a crouch, one arm clutched around his stomach.

"Well, you think you're pretty smart, don't you? Don't you? Hey, I'm talking to you!"

"No, sir. Not pretty smart." Isaac was still gasping for breath.

"No, Coach."

"No, Coach."

"Okay now, stand up here with me and look at those guys. That's what a real man is." He turned and watched Ed LaCroix spiral the ball with deadly accuracy into the arms of Jimmy Kelly, the end, who stumbled on his own feet and dropped it. "Come on, you punks, get on that ball. What the hell's the matter with you? Back up your man," he shouted. But to Isaac he said, "See that pass? That was more than thirty yards, right on target. That's what a real man can do."

Isaac by now had stopped panting and stood, triumphant almost, beside the coach. He had done something, he thought, had been given a physical test and passed it. He felt for a moment different toward the coach; he felt the way he did when he was first learning piano technique and his father would nod his head slowly in approval of his progress. I did it, he said to himself. I survived them all.

They watched in silence until Buck Carey was sure the boy had his breath back.

"Okay now, wiseguy. Try a few laps around the field."

Isaac started off at a brisk trot.

"Not on the grass; on the cinder track, you horse's ass. And don't go so fast or you'll never make it."

Watching Isaac slow to the natural stride and rhythm of a track-man, Buck Carey nodded his head in approval. Yes, I'll make that fairy into a man if it kills him, he thought.

Practice was short that day, and everybody was in high spirits returning to the locker room. "Nice going," someone said to Isaac. It was Jimmy Kelly and he didn't stop, just sort of whispered it to the side as he jogged by, but at least he said it. Isaac was glad.

The noise in the locker room was tremendous. They sang in the showers and two of them were boxing; through the splashing and the tangle of legs and arms, it was impossible to see who.

"Knock it off, Ryan!" the coach shouted. It was usually Ryan who caused trouble anyway.

For the first time Isaac was not terrified by the locker room. He recognized in an obscure way that the rough talk and the shoving and the noise were a way of affirming a male companionship he had never experienced before. It had something to do with having struggled together, with having tested their bodies together and pushed them as far as they would go, with being naked together. He was at once conscious of his exhaustion and of an exhilaration at being a man among other men, naked and accepted.

He felt a hand move on his shoulder. It was not like the shoves and bumps inevitable in the packed shower room. It was gentle. He turned large, frightened eyes up to Ed LaCroix's wide grin as the quarterback tightened his grip on Isaac's shoulder, shook him a little, and said, "Nice going, man. You done real good."

Isaac tried to answer and could not. He tried to smile, but his face was frozen. He was aware only of the hand upon his shoulder and the wide grin with its small white teeth and the blond hair curling on Ed LaCroix's chest. He felt dizzy and looked down, brushing the hand from his shoulder. But it was too late. He had begun to stiffen the way he did in bed nights when he touched himself; and Ed LaCroix had seen.

Stepping out of the shower and into the footbath, Isaac foresaw everything. The coach would stare at him, there, and tell him to stay after the others left. He would be sent to the principal or the student counselor. Everyone in school would know. He could not face it. He had faced enough.

As Isaac stepped from the footbath, the coach stared at him, there, and held out a towel. "You'd better stick around after the others leave, Goldfarb." Isaac dried himself quickly, crouching so that no one would notice, but by now everyone had noticed, and the loud horseplay had fallen off.

When the others had left, Buck Carey called Isaac to his window in the wire cage. "Look, Goldfarb, I'm gonna have to report this to the student counselor. All these things get reported to the student counselor. It looks like you need some special help. Meantime I think you'd better just forget about phys ed for a while. I don't want anybody getting in trouble around here, if you get me."

Isaac nodded. He knew it would get to the student counselor. It was his fate.

Slowly he climbed the three flights of stairs to Room 24. Linda was not there, nor was Ed LaCroix. He hadn't expected they would be. Who would wait around for a queer?

Isaac had never been in Room 24, though he knew it was the senior homeroom. On an impulse now he went from desk to desk, checking papers and books, until he found Ed LaCroix's. He sat down. The seat was low for him, but he stretched his legs out on both sides of the chair in front and slouched in that professional way the football players had. Then methodically he went through the contents of the desk, tearing pages out of books, breaking the pencils that were not already broken, stabbing the ruined books with Ed's compass. After a while he took the compass and carved on the desk top, *I hate you.*

Isaac did not go home at once. He went instead to the glee club room where, having foreseen that this too would happen, he sat silent for a moment at the piano.

There were some music sheets on the rack; someone had transcribed a Bach cantata, scoring it for piano accompaniment. It was to be the glee club's Thanksgiving concert. Having struggled endless hours with the Art of Fugue, Isaac knew Bach, but his father did not like the cantatas, and so he had never played them. Sitting down to No. 57, "Selig ist der Mann," Isaac felt he was recognizing a piece he had learned ages ago. He played the cantata through, softly, tentatively, letting the music inform his hands. There were no words, just the music; but the four arias spoke through Isaac's fingers of exile and the desire for death, death's sweetness and its joy, delivery from the martyred body. He played the piece again and again until he knew it in his fingers and in his soul, and then he went home.

Karen was angry that he was late for dinner, Avram that he had missed his practice. Isaac, his voice brittle with exhaustion and determination, was stolid under their scolding. It was as if he were already disembodied.

"Do you want to hear me play?" he asked. "Do you want to hear what you have been waiting to hear?"

"Yes, play, always play," his father said, expecting no miracle. It was too late for the soul to appear.

When Isaac finished the cantata, he turned to them and saying only, "Now you know," he walked from the room. He went to the cellar and, lugging the heavy can of kerosene, walked back to the school.

He did not know, though he suspected, that his father was sitting before the piano weeping with joy and fulfillment. "My son," he said over and over. "Karen, my son. After all these years. After all my sacrifices, he plays. At last he plays. The something missing is there. My son."

His son entered the school by the door he had left ajar. He knew it would still be ajar; he had foreseen it. He climbed to the third floor, resting on the landings, changing the can of kerosene from hand to hand.

In Room 24 he splashed the kerosene methodically in a large circle, gradually narrowing the compass until he stood with the empty can at Ed LaCroix's desk. He put the can down and rested once more. After a moment he took the compass and gouged away *I hate you* and carved his name, *Isaac*, deep into the top of the desk. Now that it was nearly over he was tired. He sat there staring straight ahead for a long time.

COMPLETED WORK

"You're always trying to make things out of junk," Sylvia said. "Why are you always trying to make things out of junk?" She flicked her cigarette ash onto the floor of his studio, or rather shook her wrist when she saw that the ash was about to fall anyway. "Well, why do you?"

He pushed the flattened cans into different positions. They were soft drink cans in varying stages of corrosion. All of them had been flattened out, some by trucks in Dupont Circle, some by his sculptor's mallet, one by the feet of several small children who had stomped the can in the middle until the two ends bent over their insteps and then they played clubfoot. He had watched them from his window through the entire afternoon, and when they finally went home, he ran down the stairs and into the street where they had thrown the can, snatched it up as if he were a thief, and returned to his studio. It was a Coca-Cola can, king size. It was this can, along with several others, he was trying to position on the battered walnut dining table that served as his workbench.

"Venner?"

"Hmmm?"

"I say, why do you bother with junk? If you think you can sculpt, why don't you use stone?" She flicked more ash onto the floor.

He walked around the table and looked at the cans from another angle. His left eyebrow twitched.

"You're not a sculptor anyway. Why do you want to be a sculptor?" she said.

"Ever since I've known you, all it's been is one crazy notion after another," she said.

"Ven?" she said.

"Hmmm?"

"It's what your priests have done to you. They've made you crazy. You ought to go back to acting. Or start acting," she said.

"Venner?" she said.

"Get out."

She sat on the high stool in the corner, one heavy leg crossed over the other.

"I said get out." His left eyebrow was twitching uncontrollably, and as if in slow motion, he reached for his mallet and pointed it at her, his arm fully extended. She leaped from the stool and ran out. A moment later she put her head in the door and screamed at him, "It's your Christ that's to blame." Again she ran out, this time in tears. Venner stood exactly as he had, his arm outstretched, the mallet quivering at the stool where she had sat.

They had met two weeks earlier. He was on his way back from Mass at St. Stephen's, and she was standing in front of his steps, waiting.

"You get up early," she said. "You're an artist. I saw some stuff through the window."

He looked at her blankly.

"Well, you are, aren't you? An artist?"

"Yes."

"I thought so. I'm Sylvia Levin. I'm your new neighbor."

"Oh, really? I didn't know they'd sold . . ." He looked at the house next door, empty now as it had been for the past year.

"Not that one. *That* one." She pointed vaguely down the street. "Neighbor's a broad term. Broad, like me."

She was broad. Her face, her shoulders, her hips, everything about her was broad. She had large humorless eyes, pinched at the brow, as if she were constantly squinting. Her mouth was wide and thin, making the aquiline nose above it appear even sharper than it was. She wore no lipstick and her black hair hung straight to her shoulders. Some disease had left heavy scars in her cheeks and in the skin around her mouth.

"Broad. Right?" she said. "So can I see your studio?"

He led her up the stairs.

"Venner Martin," she read from the nameplate as she went through the door. "Venner. Some name. Listen, you just go make your coffee and I'll look around. Okay?"

Venner shook his head and went to the kitchen to make coffee.

"My God, what a place this is!" she shouted to him. "It's like a junkyard. What are you doing with the motorcycle?"

"Thinking," he shouted back.

"Well, at least your walls are neat." One of the walls was hung with tools: chisels of all shapes and sizes, drills, mallets, a small hatchet; manila pockets holding nails and screws and odd pieces of wire and wood; loops of copper tubing and woven silver metal. Everything was meticulously in place. And on a small table at the window stood a large flowerpot sprouting paintbrushes, brown and black; it was this she had seen from outside. The other wall held a shelf of books and odd bits of sculpture. Dozens of pictures stood against the baseboard, faces turned to the wall. The only furniture in the room was a high stool, heaped with old newspapers, and a huge walnut table covered with all kinds of rubbish.

She examined the sculpture idly, seeing only shapes and colors, nothing that interested her. She went over to one of the paintings and turned it face forward.

"Don't," he said, behind her.

"It's a painting. I want to see it."

It was evidently a man's back, all orange and yellow smears. After a moment she made out the eyes; he was looking over his shoulder, a blurred expression on his face, if it was meant to be a face.

"What's this?" she said.

"The scourging."

"The scourging? What do you mean?"

"It's Christ being scourged at the pillar. Second sorrowful mystery."

She dropped the painting against the wall and pushed it into place with her toe.

"I get it. Catholic."

"Mmmm."

"Well, good luck, buddy boy," she said, angry. "Good luck!" She left, slamming the door behind her.

Two days later she was back.

"Just go ahead and work," she said. "It doesn't bother me." She pushed the newspapers off the stool and climbed onto it. "Actually, it will be interesting. I've never seen an artist at work, and I'd like to verify that perspiration-inspiration ratio you keep hearing about." She lit a cigarette. "I'm in sociology, or was. Social work."

"There's a difference, you know."

She shrugged. "Just go ahead and work."

He left the room, and she heard the door creak and slam shut. A few minutes later there was a heavy bumping noise on the back stairs, and he came through the kitchen door dragging an enormous section of tree trunk. The tree had been cut immediately below and above the first branches, and a small part of the branches themselves had been left intact on the trunk. What remained was a very gnarled piece of seasoned wood, vaguely cruciform, heavy, unpromising. With a grunt he heaved it up to the table and then turned it slowly back and forth in the light. After a while he got a chair from the kitchen and sat down, examining the wood.

More than an hour passed. She sat with her chin in her hand, smoking, staring at him. He sat staring at the piece of wood.

"You're a real thrilling worker, Venner," she said, but he gave no indication whether or not he had heard her.

Some days she sat and said nothing. Others she talked endlessly.

"My A.B. is in English lit. Can you imagine that? Milton? I actually read him, everything, even the Latin poems. At C.C.N.Y. I got my M.A. in sociology from Hunter. I taught there, you know, Venner, until my collapse. Nothing dramatic. I just realized one morning on my way to class that I had nothing to say to anybody about the development of societal and social relations. So I didn't go to class that day. I went down to Horn and Hardart's and had the roast beef special and tried to feel something for the creeps and kooks that wander in and out of Horn and Hardart's. I felt as if I wanted to throw up but couldn't. You know that feeling? Well, that's how I felt. I haven't been back since. To Hunter, I mean."

Silence for a while.

"Ven? Venner?"

"Hmmm?" He was reproducing the tree's whorls and ridges on a small pad of paper. The sketches piled up next to him, the minute variations not detectable except to himself. There were more than a hundred now.

"Just checking for vital signs. What the hell are you going to do with that tree? You've been staring at it for a week now."

He put down his pencil and looked at her. "I'm trying to find out what's in it."

"No you aren't."

He picked up his pencil again.

"No you aren't. You're trying to find a way to put in it what isn't there."

"Get out," he said.

"A pleasure."

The next morning she was waiting for him as he returned from Mass.

"I'm dying for some coffee," she said. "Look!" She had a bag of Dunkin Donuts.

"Terrific," he said. "Pure protein."

Later she pushed the coffee mug away and said, "How do you live anyhow? Who supports you?"

"I do."

"How?"

"I teach. And once in a while I sell something. A little bread goes a long way. It's tools that cost."

"What do you teach? I mean, when? You're always here."

"I teach two out of three semesters at the Corcoran. One course each. This is my semester off. I earn three thousand four hundred fifty dollars. I survive."

She seemed to have lost interest suddenly. She was staring at the empty coffee cup.

"What about you?"

"What?"

"You. Who supports you?"

"Oh, Daddy does." She smiled grimly. "Daddy left me a fat little trust fund of one hundred thou. I can't touch it, but I get six thousand a year, interest."

"Nice daddy."

"Yes, he was nice. Nice and thoughtful. Got himself out, got the money out. It was just my mother and myself he seemed to overlook."

"Out?"

"Of Poland. During the war."

"My God. What happened to you?"

"What do you ask such shitty questions for? Sometimes you make me sick, Venner, you know that? Why don't you go play hide-and-seek with Jesus in that tree?"

Later, as if nothing had happened, she began to chatter away in the studio.

"Do you know what's nice about you, Venner? Your hands. You've got the most unusual hands. They aren't beautiful. I wouldn't know how to describe them. They're like instruments, do you know what I mean? I mean, they could be made of metal, precision instruments; they look like they have a life of their own. They're not a man's hands, or a woman's either, really. They're not like hands at all. They're even a different color than your face. Your face is a sort of gray, but your hands have blood in them. Do you know what I mean? Ven?"

"Mmmm."

"You've got kinky hair, like a Jew. Funny, there's almost nothing to you, is there? You must be strong, I guess, lifting that junk around, all that metal and that tree, but you don't look strong. You don't look anything."

She studied him in silence for a while. He wore a blue work shirt and jeans and the kind of boots laborers wear on construction. Beneath the shirt his chest seemed to cave in, and the jeans hung low on his thin hips. He had no masculine characteristics whatever.

"Have you ever had sex?" she said.

He went on touching the tree trunk, pressing against the wood with his thumbs, exploring.

"Ven?"

"Hmmm?"

"Have you ever had sex?"

He only looked at her.

"Well, have you? It's a perfectly straightforward question."

He continued to look at her in silence.

"You should have been an actor, you know that? You've got that wonderful blank look. You're the kind of face that is in now, too. You don't have to be handsome any more to be a star in the movies. All you've got to do is have that blank look. It makes people think they see things there."

"How come you've got no accent if you're from Poland?" His left eyebrow had begun to twitch.

"Still mulling that one, hey? Twenty years in New York, buddy boy, you lose an accent." She got off the stool and came toward him, dropping cigarette ash on his table. "I was raped by the guards eleven times in one day when I was thirteen years old. Nine were Germans. Two were Jews."

She tapped the tree trunk with a fingernail. "It's been done already, Venner. You're wasting your time."

It was on the next day that he decided to put aside the tree trunk temporarily and work instead on his junk sculpture. That was the day she ran out screaming, "It's your Christ that's to blame," and, for the first time, crying. He couldn't figure out whether she had meant Christ in heaven or Christ in the tree trunk. She had not been back since.

A week passed and Venner, working without interruption, completed a Last Supper. He took twelve soft-drink cans, rusted, torn, flattened by cars and feet and God knows what, and nailed them to a two-by-four. The tops of the cans jutted like heads above the wood, and he painted faces on them, surprised and whimsical faces, each one an individual. In the middle he nailed the king-size Coca-Cola can the kids had used to play clubfoot. Christ's face he deliberately made a blank. Let people think they see things there. It's the real thing, he said.

Suddenly he had ideas for everything. The junk lying all around the studio came alive with that special life he brought to it—not its own life, but the life it could become. From a wig dummy, a fire alarm box, and a broken doll, he constructed an Immaculate Conception. The Maji from broken umbrellas. St. Francis of Assisi from old bicycle parts, St. Joseph from brooms and dust-pans, Marys from everything. He welded the motorcycle to a metal frame and he constructed a rider from pipes, which he then covered in jeans, a helmet, and a leather jacket. Behind the rider he placed a woman made of chicken wire, wearing a backpack, cradling a child in her arms. The Flight into Egypt.

Exhausted, excited, he determined to work on the tree trunk once again. Almost immediately he saw the image emerge from the wood, and with firm decisive whacks he chiseled away a torso, the upper arms wrenched painfully in the joints. One arm was higher than the other, and the neck bulged slightly with the grain of the wood as it ran into the shoulder. Even without the face, there was a look of agony in the body, cut off at the chest, the stubs of arms twisted in their sockets.

He postponed doing the face until he thought more about it. He studied, as he had done all his life, the faces of Christ in the earliest frescoes, the Byzantine Christs, the Medieval, the Renaissance. None of them were right for what he wanted to do. He began to search photographic books, pictures of the poor, the starving, blacks. And then he stumbled on the records of the Nuremberg trials, with the photographs of women herded naked to the extermination showers, the haunted faces behind the wire, the heaps of children's shoes. He could not, he would not, use Sylvia's face. Once again he put aside the sculpture temporarily.

"I'm going back," she said. "I'm all done in Washington." She had appeared at his door one morning with the news of her departure. "So what about a cup of coffee?"

She walked around the studio, poking at things on the table, picking up a strip of lace, a two-way plug, a broken pencil. She saw the unfinished Christ on the Cross, but said nothing until Venner came back into the room.

"I see you've made some progress with the spook in the tree."

"It's coming along."

"I thought you'd have finished it by now. I thought you'd have used my face."

They drank their coffee in silence for a while.

"Would you have liked that?" he said.

"It would be the first pock-marked Jesus."

There seemed to be no more to say.

"Go ahead and work. It won't bother me. I just came to say goodbye. I'm off to New York."

"How come?"

"Work's done."

"What's that supposed to mean?"

"It's a euphemism. It means I'm out of money."

"What about the six thousand? Have you been living that high down here?"

"What six thousand?"

"From your father. The trust fund."

"Oh, that."

"Well, what about it?"

"I just made that up. There isn't any trust fund."

"You made it up! Did you make it all up? The camp, the rapes, the whole thing?"

"No, that's true. Oh, I get it. Don't worry, you won't lose your face."

"Face?"

"For your tree trunk there."

"How am I supposed to know what's true and what's not true?"

"That's called living, buddy boy. Listen to this. When I was twelve I was going to a convent school in Poland. They had me registered there as a Catholic because they were rounding up Jews for the ovensies. Nobody knew I was Jewish, of course. So one day we were all marched into chapel to go to confession and I told the nun I couldn't do it and she asked me why and I told her. She said, 'Just tell Father what you told me,' and I did. I said, 'I'm Jewish, Father, so I can't go to confession,' and do you know what he did? He got out of his box and pulled the curtain aside from where I was kneeling and then he grabbed me by the arm and brought me straight out of church and handed me over to a Nazi guard. Straight from there to the camp."

"That's a lot of crap."

"Is it?"

"For one thing, what was a Nazi guard doing at the school? Patrolling confessions?"

"They knew somebody was a Jew. They just didn't know it was me."

"Crap."

"Goodbye, Venner. Hope the work goes well."

She stood and slowly lit a cigarette, dropping the match to the floor. She walked over and looked for a long minute at the uncompleted sculpture. She tapped the blank face as she had once before and said, "It's been done, you know, Venner."

"She'll be back," he said aloud to the empty room. "She'll be back, the lying bitch."

He began to have nightmares about his work. He was in a gallery on opening night. A huge sign at the entrance announced "Junk Sculpture by Venner Martin." There were rooms and rooms of his work, each piece perfectly displayed, labeled, dated. People walked aimlessly, consulting their programs, smiling at the sculpture. Venner moved from place to place until, attracted by laughter, he found himself in a small room without windows. In the center stood a large marble pillar, and on top of it his unfinished sculpture of Christ on the Cross. Beneath the work was a neatly labeled card that said, "Ultimate Junk." Everyone was laughing wildly, malicious laughter, and he could not walk away.

He dreamed sometimes that he had completed the sculpture. Christ's head tipped slightly to the side and, above the twisted shoulders, his face mirrored betrayal and abandonment. His eyes were large and humorless, pinched at the brow. His mouth was wide and thin, making the aquiline nose above it appear sharper than it was. There were scars on his cheeks and around his mouth. It was Sylvia's face.

They were in his studio and he had given her the sculpture as a gift.

"It's mine to keep?"

"It's yours."

"You know what I'm going to do with it, of course."

"Yes."

"And still you say it's mine."

"Yes."

She took the small hatchet that hung on the wall and with carefully aimed blows hacked away the nose and the eyes and the pitted cheeks. She did it calmly, slowly, and then she embraced the ruined figure, weeping.

Sometimes in the dream they both attacked the sculpture, and when they were done they made love, fiercely, ridiculously, among the chips of wood on the floor.

He was sure she would come back.

In time his nightmares grew less frequent and then stopped altogether. He let the sculpture stand on the table for a while and then he moved it to a corner, its empty face turned from the room.

He began to give more of his time to teaching, and at the beginning of the second semester moved his Christ into the backyard. He put it, with other uncompleted work, under the steps where it would be out of the way.

By the end of the year he had decided to give up sculpting temporarily and to concentrate on his teaching. Teaching was good for him, he thought. And besides, he was respected at school for the precision of his judgments. He liked teaching. It made him feel complete, more or less.

THE PLUMBER

HE ALWAYS sat in the park. It wasn't really a park, it was more a
fenced-in green, but he called it the park. It was cooler than his
rooms and sometimes other people came to sit and, besides, where
else could he go? So Mr. Ransom sat there every day watching
everything that happened, and within two days forgot everything
he had watched. This way of living provided him with endless
stimulation; everything he saw was fresh and new and interesting. It was inevitable, therefore, that since he was eighty,
many would think him mad.

The park was a tattered affair people passed through on their
way somewhere else—to shop or to work or to shorten the distance
between Cambridge Street and Broadway. It was a gloomy place
with patches of grass here and there, and a fountain that no longer
worked, and a few benches. Few people except the old man ever
sat there.

Saturdays were best in the park. That is, they were the nearest
thing to summer, which was really the best. You could always plan
on plenty of excitement Saturdays, what with young girls—it was
impossible now to guess how young, they all wore such grown-up
clothes—bringing back books to the library and lingering in the
park to say hello to their boy friends. And the fathers who brought
their children to play in the grass while they themselves did their
homework; they were students at Harvard, no doubt. The women
gossiping. That fine young man with the St. Bernard. The Jesuit
from across the way who was growing a beard and who, when he
spoke, always said such pleasant things, even though all the un-

happiness of the world was in his eyes. Regina, who never came except on Saturdays. The crazy lady with her bag of cookies. The lady with her pocket Pekingese, the man with his two corgis, the professor with his astounding parrot. Saturdays were best in the park—except for summer.

In summer there were children every day and, even though he couldn't see Tim Keefe's house with the garden in front, there was splendor enough right in front of him. The baby squirrels played their antic games, foolishly freezing in position while a dog sniffed them all around, and then off terrified to a tree. And the birds, some fledglings and some mother birds, squawking and chirping and carrying on. And the dogs: the yellow mongrel with the crooked leg, the St. Bernard whose name was Abelard, the big black Labrador, the crazy brown and black dog that ran whimpering through the park, snapping at everyone who got in his path. Even the other dogs made way for him. What else? The swans singing in the trees when the sun shimmered through the sticky new leaves, but of course that was an illusion, he knew that. The glorious trees: maples, oaks, an elm in the corner near the library. The flowers, there were only three little clusters of iris, but they were an unusual gold and purple, a heraldic device beside the cement fountain. The grass, each blade honed to a green perfection. And the weeds, no ordinary weeds, but dandelions and crab grass and, near the fence, a beautiful ragweed.

This was how he saw his park. This was how it was. He had been a plumber all his life, and his words and thoughts had always been ordinary; only his vision was strange.

* * *

Attix Ransom was not born in Cambridge. He had come there late one summer afternoon, a baby of two years, so that when he grew up he might attend Harvard. That was his aunt's idea which, along with most of her ideas, was never realized. All of his ancestors had gone to Harvard, and Margaretta Susan Ransom, having determined that her ward would go there also, sold what little remained of the family inheritance and rented a tiny apartment in Cambridge, where she became renowned for her fine sewing. She died when Attix was fifteen and had only just been apprenticed to a plumber. It was the plumbing, her friends said, that killed her.

Attix Cornelius Ransom was the great-grandson of the richest man Louisiana had ever known. He owned not one but several adjoining cotton plantations, staffed by darkies he had never succeeded in counting, and he was an importer as well. Though he began life poor, the times and the land and the swelling slave trade made him a fortune, which doubled each year. When in 1863 he died at a small town in Pennsylvania, "fighting to protect our slaves," he had said, his wealth miraculously remained intact in the hands of his son, Jason Cornelius Ransom. Miraculously, that is, insofar as the son's ability to bribe, cheat, and swindle Yankee and nigger alike could be termed miraculous. Jason fathered and reared seven children amid fantastic wealth, which did not prepare them for the financial annihilation that followed the long night of August 14, 1888, when their father gambled away every boll of cotton and stick of furniture they owned and then, being a gentleman, put a bullet through his head. His eldest son, Cornelius Attix Ransom, who had never worked and had never expected to work, found himself before the end of that same month the father of a child whose mother had died in labor. Cornelius named the child after its great-grandfather, Attix Cornelius Ransom, in the dim hope that he might reestablish the family fortune. Two years later, confused and rambling in his mind, Cornelius Attix Ransom also died, and the baby fell to the care of Margaretta, who took him to Cambridge, where he grew up and became a plumber.

He had heard the story of the decline and fall of the Ransoms often enough. At first it fired his imagination; he hoped to grow up to be a poet, and the romantic grandfather who put a bullet through his head after he had wrecked the family fortune seemed to justify this vocation. Later he thought he might prefer to be an artist, words having proved recalcitrant somewhere around the eighth grade, but that too was impractical, since oils and canvas cost so much.

Hard-working and unimaginative, he became in time a plumber valued for his skill and efficiency. His work was his life, except on

Sundays when he took long walks, on one of which he met Kathleen Riordan. She was charmed by the notion of a plumber with such a name as Attix Cornelius Ransom, and her parents were pleased that their plain, broad-faced daughter had found a man who didn't drink and had a fine steady income, and she nearly thirty now with all hope of marriage gone. They were not pleased at his being a Protestant. Religion had never mattered to Attix anyway and so he entered the Catholic Church, attending Mass faithfully every Sunday for the forty years of their marriage, and after Kathleen's death and burial never attending again. He had done it for her and she needed it no longer, he felt, but he remained well disposed toward the Sisters and the clergy in general.

His marriage had been rich. The plain Kathleen loved him with a passion that had waited nearly thirty years for someone on whom to lavish it. She bore him a son, Cornelius, whom they called Neil, and when she was over forty a daughter named Kathleen. Neil went to Harvard, where the clarity of his thought and precision of expression marked him early as the important lawyer he would later become. During his college years Neil never admitted his father was a plumber; that he should have such a background seemed to him somehow unfair. Kathleen, who began life with the Riordan face, blossomed unexpectedly into the Ransom beauty, and in her senior year at Radcliffe married her history professor and moved to California. He loved his children, since they were the reflections of his single-minded love for his wife, but he loved them only vaguely. The center of his existence was his Kathleen, more plain and more broad-faced as she aged, and when she died, his own life ended. He was seventy, two years younger than she; he sold the house and moved into the tiny apartment on Trowbridge Street, where he waited to die. Meanwhile he went to sit in the little park he could see from his bedroom window. He had been going there for ten years, and now he was eighty, and not dead yet.

*   *   *

Attix Ransom was a permanent figure in the park. People expected him to be there as they expected equestrian statues to be in the Boston Common. He was in a very minor way an institution, seated on the bench with his hands folded, face smiling with pleasure at the things he saw.

He would arrive at ten in the morning with his little brown package and sit where the sun would strike him full in the face. The young women came by on their way to the laundromat, some pushing a huge sack of bedlinen in a baby carriage, some carrying it slung over their shoulders as if they were peasants bringing in the harvest. One had a golf cart. The Jesuit came by and stopped to talk for a moment; it was hard to guess what his work might be, since twice a day he ambled through the park on what was clearly a walk. Who but retired old men take strolls twice a day, he wondered. The lady with the Pekingese came by, shot him the look of mistrust she had for ten years practiced on him, and when her dog had done its toilet, jerked at its leash and led it away. She was such a cross woman, he told himself, and said it not as judgment or condemnation but in wonder at the variety of human personalities.

At noon he would open his package and eat the grinder he bought each morning at the little food store over which he had his apartment. He ate only half of it, carefully wrapping the other half in the brown paper to eat with some soup for his dinner. He enjoyed the grinders, there were at least six different kinds, and they made cooking unnecessary.

After his lunch, he walked several times around the low wire fence that enclosed the park, allowing himself as much as an hour to gaze on the wonder of the Tim Keefe garden. It was a garish affair, three feet wide and nine feet long, into which were crowded four display tables. There was a cement birdbath, on top of which a plaster pixie lifted her skirts from the water. There was a pile of three cement blocks supporting an enamel basin, which overflowed with petunias; rising from the little sea of flowers was a rosy-cheeked Lady of Lourdes. There was a low stepladder painted silver, each step groaning with huge clay pots of petunias. There was a cafeteria table on which sat an enormous plaster frog; a sequined net around him dripped almost to the ground; hanging from his neck was a string of glass pendants from an old chandelier. The little ground that remained was a mass of petunias

and geraniums, flowers that in fall were replaced by chrysanthe-
mums, some real and some plastic, and by jars of crimson
broomgrass. The garden was something of a neighborhood joke,
something everyone stopped to look at for any number of reasons.
Mr. Ransom had only one reason; it was surpassingly beautiful.

Standing at the garden, he could shift his gaze to the left and
admire the sign above the door. It was an enormous sign in red
and white, proclaiming that this was the home of Tim Keefe, Hall
of Fame pitcher for the New York Giants. Above the sign, propped
on a table, a carousel horse galloped into the air, a monkey astride
his back holding a little banner that once again proclaimed Tim
Keefe.

Shifting his gaze to the right, he could marvel at the Costa Funeral Home; they were tearing it down now, a hazard to children
ever since the fire there. But for the past ten years it had occupied as much of his attention as the garden.

A vast Venetian palace of stucco and green brass, it was faced
on the first floor with innumerable marble pillars set into niches
every few feet. The second floor was cream-colored, with bits of
turquoise glass forming geometric patterns directly above the pillars below. The top floor was a series of cupolas and arches and
domes. But the amazing feature of the house was the glass porch
that stood above the entrance and extended almost to the side-
walk. Attix always expected to see candles burning there and
women with long black veils kneeling. In fact, no funeral proces-
sion had ever gone in or out of the house, nor were there ever
lamps lit in the front parlors. There was something unpleasantly
peculiar about the house, so out of place in its environment, so
out of time. At night people walked more rapidly as they passed
it, and in the day boys would sometimes throw stones at the back
windows. But since the fire, they were tearing it down.

After his walk and his meditation, Attix Ransom returned to
his bench, where he would sit motionless for hours, thinking of
the wonders he had only now looked upon. The children never
bothered him any more. They had at one time.

They would run by him shouting, "Old Mr. Pee-the-Bed, Old
Mr. Pee-the-Bed," giggling insanely all the while. After weeks of
this and he never responding, one of the braver boys—he was ten—

stopped in front of him and said, "Ha, ha, you're so poor you eat only half a sandwich." The others behind him picked up their cue and chanted, "Ha, ha, you're so poor," over and over until finally the old man's confusion cleared and he realized they hated him. To the boy who stood before him, hands on hips, legs spread, challenging, he extended the half grinder. He smiled. The boy was suddenly frightened—feeling as he had that time after setting fire to a cat—and, uncertain of what his friends expected from him, he took the package, ran a little distance, and then in a fury threw it at the man. It struck him in the temple, peppers and bits of sausage splattering his clothes. He hung his head and said nothing. After that day none of the children ever bothered him again.

At seven or even eight he went home; in the fall he went earlier. He heated the soup and ate it and then, having poured himself a tumbler of bourbon, he would settle into the newspaper, reading everything and marveling, forgetting what he had read as easily as he forgot what he had seen.

Thus his day was full with things seen and done; he had his park and his rooms above the food store, and he had his visions.

* * *

When Attix had first moved into the little apartment, Neil had driven up from Hartford, agitated and embarrassed at his father's excessive grief. He worried that the old man could not get along by himself, and offered to hire a woman who would come in and cook at least the evening meal for him. But Attix would not hear of it, going so far as to lie to his son that in the past several years he had often done the cooking when Kathleen was feeling poorly and there was no reason on earth he couldn't continue to do so. Neil continued to worry, however, especially when with the passage of years something seemed to be happening to his father's mind. He wandered. He seemed almost whimsical at times. He would speak of things that had happened many years ago as if they had happened yesterday and, more alarming, speak of something recent—a riot on some college campus—as if it had occurred sixty years ago and he alone preserved the memory of it. Senility was harmless enough, but in an old man living by himself it could be dangerous. Neil and his wife therefore visited him every second Sunday between two and five o'clock. Recently they had begun looking into the question of a nursing home, not knowing his devotion to his park or the regular occurrence of wonders that made life beautiful to him.

It was a Sunday in fall when they decided the time had come to look after the poor soul properly. They made the decision after listening to his animated conversation, more vague and rambling than they had ever heard it, noting for the first time that his thoughts had become quite incoherent.

Neil had again brought up the matter of his father's leaving the apartment for a nursing home, where he would have proper care and where he could be with people his own age.

"It must be terribly lonely for you here, Dad. For instance, what did you do yesterday?"

Attix paused for a moment, thinking why should I tell him?

* * *

Yesterday, like every day this fall, had been perfect. You can smell the fall, he said to himself, there's something in the leaves, the beautiful colored leaves. Even the grass seemed sweeter. There is nothing so beautiful as fall. Nothing.

"Well, hello!"

"Hello! Oh yes, hello!" He rubbed his hands and smiled at the young priest.

"Well, you've certainly got another beautiful day here."

"Oh yes. It's always beautiful in the park." He looked at the young man's eyes. A priest, he thought, and so sad, as if he had seen something too awful to tell about. "Your beard. It's turning into a fine beard."

For a while the Jesuit stood there saying nothing, though it was unlike him to stand still. "Our house is almost down," he said.

"Our house. Yes, it's too bad. It was a beautiful house in its time."

"It was still beautiful. *Still*, it was beautiful." He spoke as if he were angry. "People always have to destroy whatever is beautiful when they can't understand it." He turned and looked at the

house and then turned back. "I'll tell you what, Mr. Ransom.
When they finish wrecking it, when they've destroyed it completely,
I'll join you here for lunch and I'll bring a bottle of wine and we
can cheer each other up. Okay?" He spoke as if it were less an
invitation than a challenge.

"Oh yes. Oh, that will cheer us up."

"Do you like wine? What kind do you like?"

"Wine?" Attix never drank wine. "Oh, I drink any kind. I like
sweet wine."

"Sweet wine and grinders. Next week. You won't forget now.
Everything depends on it." The young man stood staring at the
old one; he seemed to have something difficult to say.

"Yes, yes," Attix muttered, "your beard is fine."

"God bless you, Mr. Ransom. And thank you." He walked away,
and for a moment Attix thought he was crying. A sad, nervous
young man.

Squirrels made the morning short, gathering acorns, skittering
up and down the tree trunks. And then the man with the two
corgis came by. They were old dogs and aristocratic and so did
not condescend to sniff about after the squirrels or even to be
distracted by them. They padded by, superior to everything around
them, satisfied with their own doggy perfection, Attix thought.
Look at them, the richest dogs in Louisiana, studying at Harvard,
no doubt.

All morning there was a steady file of girls and boys going to
the library. So many interesting faces, so many of them foreign—
Oriental, he thought. And then just after lunch, Regina came.

"I'm in school this year. I go to school." She climbed up on the
bench beside him. She had never done this before; though she
saw him regularly on Saturdays, she was generally shy and stood
at a distance peeking at him through her hair.

"Well, now. Isn't that nice! Do you like school, Regina?"

"Yes. Miss Foley is a big fat lady with teeth like this and she's
very nice." Regina made her front teeth protrude in imitation of
Miss Foley's.

He laughed, and she continued to make the face.

She climbed down from the bench, looked at him a moment,

climbed back up and, putting her mouth against his ear, whispered: "I love you," and ran away.

A sweet little girl, he thought. Feeling almost guilty that his life was so full, he closed his eyes and, drowsy in the sun, fell momentarily asleep. He awoke with a start. Afternoon light was pouring through the brown and golden leaves; there was a swan floating on dark water, and beyond the trees the ocean stretched out forever. He heard someone speaking.

> Lovelier than April rain or sullen pain's surcease
> Is the dark I live: the cool caress of leaves
> Against my face in autumn, foam nets the ocean weaves
> And casts about my feet, the wild swans crying peace.

The voice was familiar because it was his own. He looked about and then, reassured to find himself alone, laughed softly at his embarrassment. It was a poem, he said. I was reciting a poem. He tried to think where he had heard it, but of course he had not heard it anywhere; he had said it.

Saturday was a full day. He was not able to spend a whole hour at the Tim Keefe garden, and only out of deep concern was he able to contemplate the near-ruins of the funeral home. The hippies, people said, had been holding love-ins or smoke-ins or something harmless there, and eventually the place had been gutted by fire. A love-in, he said to himself, and stared with affection at the first floor of the house, since that was all that remained. It would soon be level with the ground and they would make it a parking lot or, more likely, erect a glassy new apartment building, which would be nice in its way but not the same as something old and odd and loved for what it had been as well as for what it was.

Well, everything passes, oh yes, he said, and returned to his rooms above the food store, where he heated his soup and ate it and waited with no anticipation for his son's visit on the following day.

*   *   *

When Neil asked him what he had done yesterday, Attix Ransom paused for a moment, thinking. Why should I tell him? he thought. Why should I share something he cannot, for all his lawyer's understanding, grasp at all? That life is not just having . . . and then from nowhere he heard Kathleen's voice saying, "Because he is your son. Because he is our son." And so for Kathleen's sake, he told him.

"Yesterday?" he said. "Yes, oh yes. Let me see, yesterday." He looked into his son's eyes; they were patient and encouraging and loving, but they had already made a decision. He looked at his daughter-in-law, a beautiful girl once, but hard about the mouth now. She was flicking bits of imaginary lint from her fashionably long skirt. "Yesterday," he said again. They are my children, our children. I will give them the only thing I have left.

"Yesterday, like all the days this fall, was perfect. After I had cleaned the house and kissed your mother, because I miss her so, because I love her, I left for the park. My park. It was fresh and alive there. In fall nothing dies, everything changes, and everything in the park was changing right before my eyes. The trees, the beautiful trees, and the cool caress of leaves against my face, the swans were singing, crying peace and peace and then the Jesuit came by. We are going to have a picnic when the house is down. Not to rejoice, you understand, oh no, but to cheer each other up. He's growing a beard and will bring some wine, sweet wine, and we will drink it in the park to cheer each other up.

"It was the same when your mother died. I understand. You can live with only so much loss, and then you turn to anything. Anything at all. He turned to me, the young man, the priest, and he said, 'When they've destroyed it completely, I'll join you here for lunch and we can cheer each other up.' You would understand if you could see him. His eyes. I don't know what he has seen, but all the light in them is gone. But that was the sad part.

"There were other things. The girl came by, so sweet with her long hair and her smile. Regina. She told me that she loved me and, do you know, she does. A little girl. The corgis, going to Harvard. And the Orientals played croquet, a noisy group, but happy and alive with the soft wind and the leaves falling.

"Later I went by the garden. The carousel horse made me think of when you were little, Neil, and we were at the circus, at a gambling booth, and suddenly a gun went off. I said to your mother,

'Grandfather has shot himself and we are ruined.' But ruin isn't ever what it seems. Never. And we went home. So I didn't stay very long at the garden, but thought about the house instead.

"Your thoughts ramble, you know, when you get old, and I was thinking of the house. The columns and the stained glass and next-door diamonds trickling from the bullfrog's perch. It was sad, torn down for a love-in, or whatever it is they do. I came home and warmed my soup, thinking I will have some sweet wine with the Jesuit who is mad, poor young man, who needs someone to have wine with and a grinder."

Attix Cornelius Ransom stopped then and smiled at his son and his daughter-in-law.

"Well," he said, "there you are. That is all there is."

They said goodbye to the old man, and when they reached Hartford made arrangements for St. Luke's Home for the Aged to take the poor old soul, which they agreed to do within the week.

* * *

They came for him on Sunday. He had not gone to the park since Friday morning, when they had called to tell him he would be admitted to the Home that week. Nor had he eaten. He had sat at the window of his bedroom looking out over the park and watching the daily destruction of the funeral home.

I am leaving forever, he thought. I will never see the park again.

Sunday was difficult for everyone. Neither Neil nor his wife spoke on the trip up to Cambridge, both feeling somehow guilty. They were convinced they were doing the right thing; still, it made them uncomfortable.

As for Attix himself, he had brooded for the past three days about the poor young Jesuit who would be looking for him but would not find him in the park. When his son arrived, he explained this, but to no effect, since Neil kept assuring him that the priest would understand. Mr. Ransom shook his head and climbed into the car.

The house had been razed on Saturday. The next day the Jesuit, nervous but smiling and armed with an hour's conversation, came to the park with his bottle of sweet wine. For months he had been taking therapeutic walks at his psychiatrist's insistence and now, for the first time in his life, he had proposed a meeting with another human being. The young priest waited for two hours and then went home, where he sat staring at the wall, clenching and unclenching his fists until it was time for him to go downstairs to his silent dinner. Twice during the meal he muttered, "Never! Never!" But by that time both Attix and his son were preoccupied with other things.

The heavy car swung on to Massachusetts Avenue, and from there onto a series of turnpikes that would take them quickly and efficiently to the nursing home. There was no conversation. In the back seat Attix continued with himself the dialogue of the past three days, asking himself what would happen to him and where he was going.

Sun was pouring in the window against which his head bobbed as he drifted into sleep. The sun. The beautiful sun making swans sing in the trees and the ocean ribbed with foam, but stretching out to where the sea went black until Regina came walking across the water to him, climbed into his lap, and whispered, "I love you." And then the Jesuit was there, smiling, sad. "I've brought you wine, sweet wine, because the house is down."

"Yes," Attix said, "that will cheer us up. But I can't stay. I'd like to stay, but I can't."

"Where are you going?" the Jesuit said, and he was angry.

"Didn't you know? I thought you would know," the old man said. "I have to die. I'm dying."

"No you're not," the Jesuit said. "It's not that easy. It never is." And he gripped Mr. Ransom by the wrist, very hard.

"But the swans, the ocean."

The Jesuit brought his face very close to the old man's. "It's survival that costs," he said, and the ferocity of his stare dragged Mr. Ransom back into life. "Dying is the easy way."

The car pulled to a smart stop in front of the nursing home. It was a huge building of white stone, and it glittered in the sun like a block of ice. From the back seat Mr. Ransom looked at it and shook his head once.

The Mother Superior herself came hurriedly down the steps to greet the distinguished lawyer and his father.

"Mr. Ransom," she said. "What a pleasure! Welcome to St. Luke's!" Then after a moment she said to Neil, confidentially, as if Mr. Ransom were not present, "Oh, he's so distinguished-looking. He looks just like that poet."

"No," he said, "I'm a plumber." And leaving them, he ascended the steps to the huge stone building thinking, even this will end. Even this.

BENJAMIN

A MONTH AFTER his father died, Julian began to feel constant pain beneath his left arm. He was short of breath, and often during the night he ran a fever. Heart trouble, the doctor said, and sent him to a specialist, who ran an impressive battery of tests on him, all of which proved negative. By this time Julian had begun having stomach pains and occasional nausea, so the relieved heart specialist sent him to another specialist, this one in internal medicine. Again a battery of tests proved negative. Julian was a young man, a lawyer in his midtwenties, with no history of illness and no obvious psychological problems; the three doctors concluded he was suffering from nerves. They gave him tranquilizers and pronounced him well.

To Julian's surprise, the tranquilizers seemed to work; the pains subsided, and the nausea went away altogether. He was surprised because he suspected there was a great deal wrong with him other than nerves. His suspicion ripened into certainty until finally, without telling Anne, he went to a psychiatrist and told him what he had told none of the other doctors: that ever since his father's death, he had a horror of making love.

The psychiatrist smiled and nodded his head.

Julian was unable to explain what he meant by horror. He wanted to make love, he said, but he was afraid. But afraid wasn't the right word either. He felt a terrific revulsion, he said, as if death were in the room, as if he were holding death in his arms. Immediately he began to protest that he loved his wife, that their sex life was very good, that he had begun to feel this way only recently. And even now he didn't feel this way all the time. When they made love during the day, it was fine. It was only at night that he had this horror, this . . . and he shook his head, unable to describe what he felt.

Julian saw the psychiatrist through June and July. Julian traced his family history and his own many times over, relating grim memories and happy ones in greater detail each time, coming no closer to an understanding of what his horror of lovemaking really meant. He was thinking of giving up therapy altogether when August came and the psychiatrist went on vacation. Freed from chasing after his secret self, Julian felt expansive, and proposed to Anne that they go back to London to see Benjamin.

Two years earlier on their first trip to London, neither of them had liked cats and so, apart from feeding him a tin of Sainsbury's each day, they had paid no attention to Benjamin. They were on their honeymoon and noticed nothing except each other. Then one morning they woke and made love and Anne said that while he took his bath she would go downstairs and start breakfast. Benjamin was asleep outside the door and when she opened it, he stretched luxuriously, rolling over on his back, curling in a ball, and sitting up finally with one paw over an eye.

"Poor thing," Anne said, "with nobody to love you." She bent to pat his head and Benjamin arched his back, rubbing against her and purring. "Come on, I'll feed you," she said, and started down the stairs.

Julian heard her laughter and came out on the landing.

"Look at this," Anne said. "She thinks she's a dog."

"He."

"Look."

Benjamin stood on the carpeted stairs, his body across Anne's foot, and whenever Anne forced her way down to the next step, the cat turned on his back and slid head downward to the step below. And then he would stand, purring, and throw his body against her foot once more. When they reached the bottom he streaked across the tile floor to the kitchen. It was the beginning of their love affair with Benjamin.

And now after two years of marriage they were going back to

find once more in London a civilized way of life, and to get a rest, and to see Benjamin. Most of all to see Benjamin.

They opened the door, and there he was. Before Anne could get in the house, Benjamin was rubbing his head and back against her legs, flopping on his side and wriggling, purring all the while.

"Sweet kitty," she said, and stroked his back over and over. "She's been waiting at the door for two years now, haven't you, poor Benjy?"

"Hullo, catty," Julian said, becoming British. Benjamin allowed himself to be patted by Julian and then went back to rubbing against Anne.

"You're hungry, aren't you, Benj? Well, I'm going to give you some lovely food. Come on."

At the word food, Benjamin patted away to the kitchen and took up his station at the refrigerator. Anne was emptying the tin of cat food into the blue ceramic dish when she heard Julian calling from the bedroom above.

"The Hills left a note, hon. They say that he's to have only half a tin a day. He's on a desperate diet."

"I've already given her a whole one."

"Mrs. Hill says the vet says it's imperative. Imperative. She's got it underlined."

"Well . . ."

He couldn't hear the rest.

"What?"

"I said Benjy's on vacation too. He's celebrating our anniversary."

"Come on up here and *we'll* celebrate."

"Why don't you go to bed? You should go to bed, your famous nerves and all."

"Come up here."

She came down the hall from the kitchen and saw him standing naked on the lower landing.

"Julian, for God's sake, people can see you through that window."

"I can't keep this up forever."

"Pig. I married a pig," she said.

"It's your big chance. Ta-rah!"

"Honestly, why are you so damned perverse? You never want to have sex under the most normal conditions, and then when we get off the plane and are both dying of jet lag or whatever you call it, you decide it's the time to get cute." She had meant to joke, but the words came out serious.

"Nine, eight, seven . . ."

"Get away from that window," she said, and ran up the stairs. After they made love, they lay side by side looking at the ceiling. For a long time neither said anything.

"It's going to be a good trip, isn't it," she said.

"Yes, I'm really going to try."

"If you can just put your worries out of your mind, you know? It's because you're always thinking about them."

"What do you mean, worries?"

"Well, you know. Your pains in the chest and then the stomach trouble. The doctors *said* there's nothing wrong with you."

"Maybe it's up here," he said, tapping his forehead. He wanted to tell her about seeing the psychiatrist.

"No, it's just your nerves. What you need is some sleep instead of getting up and reading half the night."

"Maybe I should see a shrink."

"That's ridiculous. People like us don't go to shrinks. We see what has to be done and we do it. Period. Shrinks are for people who live miserable lives because they're afraid to hurt anybody."

"Where'd you get all that?"

"Partly I thought it and partly I got it from Bill."

Bill was Anne's brother, a priest.

"Yeah, well, he needs one."

"He goes to one."

"He should."

"He does. But you're not like him. Neither am I. As soon as you decide to stop worrying that you're dying, the pains will go away. You're probably identifying with your father."

"Bullshit."

They rolled over and lay back to back.

"I'm sorry I mentioned your father. I apologize."

"It doesn't matter."

"Are you mad?"

"Well, what the hell do you know about how I feel about my father? He had good points and bad points, and he's dead. And I am *not* identifying with him."

"I know it. That was stupid of me."

"Let's not fight. We're just beginning a vacation."

They rolled over and lay face to face.

"I love you," she said, burrowing.

She was just beginning to fall asleep when Julian said, "I'm going down and sit in the sunroom and read for a while. Okay?"

She would have said no, but at the moment she felt she was on the defensive.

"I'll get up too."

"No," he said, bending over to kiss her. "You sleep."

"Do you mind?" Her eyes were closed, her lips barely moved. "Sleep."

At the door he turned and looked at her. He thought of waking her, of making love again right away, or in the sunroom maybe, on the floor. But no, she needed sleep after the flight.

We see what has to be done and we do it, he said to himself as he went down the stairs. O would some power the giftie gi'e us to see ourselves as others see us.

He sat in the wicker basket chair staring out into the garden. It was a beautiful garden, typically English. A square of thick green grass was bordered by sweet peas and geraniums. Some purple flowers with long thick petals tangled with the roses and hollyhocks that clung against the walls enclosing the garden. A huge tree stood to the right, its branches weighted with hundreds of hard green pears. There were small birds in the bushes, and the sun poured into the garden and into the little room where he sat by the glass doors that ran from floor to ceiling.

Next door a gang of boys were playing some kind of noisy game that involved throwing or kicking a soccer ball against one of the garden walls. He could hear their shouts, could tell they were very young.

He felt cozy. He felt at home.

This was his favorite room in the house, though certainly it was the strangest. The other rooms were crammed with antiques, Victorian stuff mostly, chairs of fruitwood and prickly mohair, small round tables and heavy ornamented cabinets, tiny paintings, massive frames. But the sunroom was from another age entirely. The walls were stark white, and cold. A small piano stood in one corner, a stack of sheet music piled on the floor next to it. A packing crate held some tattered paperback books and a clay cat one of the children had made. Toys were everywhere. They had thought at first it was a playroom until they realized that the large pine table flanked on either side by long benches was the only dining table in the house. There was no other furniture in the room, except the basket chair, wicker, with no cushion. The room managed to be at once modern and barbaric.

He began to feel drowsy in the warm sun. He shifted lower in the chair, propping his head against the hard wooden frame. Benjamin appeared outside the glass doors, curled up on the step, changed his mind, and moved to the stone slab that served as a potting bench. Despite his diet, the cat was still very fat. Watching him, Julian said aloud, "Oh blessed Benjamin, no tranquilizers for you." He continued to gaze out at the garden. If it weren't for the intermittent shouts of the boys next door, he might fall asleep himself, he thought. He was still thinking this an hour later when he awoke.

He was chilly. The long shadow of the pear tree had fallen across the glass doors and he shivered in the cool room. He rubbed his neck and then the sore spot at the back of his skull where it had rested on the hard wood. He leaned forward, about to stand up, when suddenly something large and gray fell into the center of the green lawn. It was a pigeon, so large that Julian laughed aloud when he realized what it was. Another pigeon joined the first. They seemed to drop from the sky, plummeting into the garden as if their weight were too much for wings to sustain.

Julian was watching the pigeons attack the fallen pears, plunging their beaks deep into the rotting fruit and tearing, when suddenly he saw Benjamin slink from the stone slab to the step and across the grass in one swift, fluid motion. He would not have thought Benjamin could move like that. He laughed again; the picture was preposterous. The pigeons were at least the size of the cat, could perhaps topple him over with one bat of the wings, and there was Benjy sneaking up on them, the jungle hunter ready to do battle for his dinner. Julian was enjoying the scene, wishing Anne were with him to enjoy it too, when suddenly he heard a loud, "Scat! Get away then." A small fat boy with red hair and short pants stood on top of the stone wall, stamping his foot loudly and shouting at the cat. The pigeons flew off, beating their heavy wings, and Benjamin came out of his hunting pose and darted into the rose bushes.

Julian studied the boy. His face was completely round and pasty white, and his head sprouted thick tufts of fiery hair. He had on short pants that were green and a strange kind of white shirt with little puffs at the shoulders. He looked like a troll in rolling breeches. Quickly he let himself down from the wall onto a compost pile and from there down into the garden. He moved around, kicking at the flowers, and then scooped up a large white soccer ball. Julian smiled at the thought of such a fat little thing playing soccer. With the ball under his arm, the boy began to call, "Here, kitty, kitty. Come on, cat." He crouched, waiting. He was very patient.

Benjamin moved from the cover of the rose bushes and settled among the sweet peas at the edge of the grass. "Here, kitty, kitty," the boy called again and again, but the cat was having none of it. Slowly the boy moved across the lawn, talking softly to the cat, nice kitty, pretty cat, until he was no more than a few feet away. Benjamin poked his nose out from among the flowers and then his whole head. One foot was just beginning to emerge when suddenly the boy raised the soccer ball high in the air and with both hands brought it hard down on the cat. The ball struck him at the base of the skull and for a moment he sprawled, both front legs flattened out on either side of his head. And then with a terrified scream he dashed from among the flowers, tore across the lawn, and disappeared into the roses on the other side of the garden.

Julian leaped to his feet and shook the glass doors, trying to get them open. They were locked, and though he twisted the key furiously back and forth, he could not open them. He ran into the kitchen and out the back door, his face burning. He wanted to get his hands on that damned little troll, he wanted to take him by the neck and thrash the life out of him, he wanted . . . But the garden was empty. There was no sign of the boy or the ball or the cat.

Julian went inside and poured himself a large drink. He concentrated on being calm. It's silly, he told himself, to fly into a rage over some perverse little kid. But then the picture came back to him, the boy with his hands above his head bringing the ball down on Benjy's head, the cat sprawled and terrified, and himself unable to open the glass doors to the garden. Julian began to get furious all over again. He sipped the drink slowly, forcing himself to think of the warm track it made through his chest into his stomach.

Later he told Anne what had happened, and she said she understood. But she did not understand. Why should a grown man, a lawyer furthermore, come apart because a kid was mean to a cat? It made no sense. It was precisely to escape that sort of insanity that they had come to London in the first place. Well, they were off to a great start. Later still, when they were in bed and she put her hand on his chest and he moved away from her, Anne said once again that she understood. And she promised herself silently that if they ever made love again it would be when Julian had become his old self once more and was desperate for it.

By the beginning of the second week they had still not made love. Almost from the first everything had gone wrong. The kid with the soccer ball. Food poisoning in an Indian restaurant in Soho. Julian with a fever, Anne vomiting. Anne with a fever, Julian vomiting. And then Walpurgisnacht, as he called it.

They were getting dressed to go out for dinner when the doorbell rang. Julian answered it, still buttoning his shirt.

"Excuse me, sir. Might we fetch our ball from your garden?"

There were three of them, about ten years old, and with that ruddy complexion and open stare that Julian liked to think typical of English children. One was considerably taller than the other two and acted as their spokesman. Julian liked the looks of them. "Just don't pester the cat," he said, and held the door for them to come through.

"Over the wall is easiest, sir," the leader said. "That is, if you don't mind."

"Sure," Julian said. "Sure." He was charmed.

He watched from the kitchen window while the boy got the ball and climbed back over the wall. He poured himself a Coke, thinking how nice English kids were, thinking he'd like to raise his own children in England.

The ball came flying over the wall. In a moment the tall boy came over after it and stood examining the windows of the house. When finally he saw Julian in the kitchen, he pointed at a pear, questioning. Julian nodded. The boy picked a pear and put it in his pocket, picked two more, and then disappeared over the wall. Almost immediately the ball was thrown into the center of the garden. Oh no, Julian said to himself. At once the three boys were in the garden. Then five. Julian went upstairs where Anne was just finishing her makeup.

"Oh my God," he said, "I don't know what I've done."

She closed her eyes in exasperation. Again, she thought. "What do you mean?" she said.

"Look."

There were seven or eight of them now going wild in the garden. One had a stick and was beating pears off the branches. They were shrieking and throwing the pears into the tree and over the garden walls.

"They're just going a little berserk. That's how kids are," she said, smiling. She taught fifth grade and knew. "They'll stop in a minute." She went back to the mirror.

"But, my God, they're really doing damage to that tree. Look, there are broken branches all over the lawn."

"They'll stop," she said. "Why don't you stop looking, for heaven's sake. You seem to want to make yourself frantic. Make us a drink, why don't you, before we go out."

He followed her down the stairs. "There's nothing worse than a grown man trying to control a crowd of kids," he said. "But what'll we tell the Hills if they wreck the garden?"

"They won't," she said. "You worry too much."

He looked out the kitchen window, though he had promised himself he would not. The garden was littered with pears and torn branches, but the boys had stopped their screaming and were gathered in one corner of the lawn. They were closing in on something, like hunters. One of them held a dead tree branch over his shoulder, and at the same moment that Julian realized he was the red-haired troll, the boys all shouted there he is, get him, and the boy with the branch brought it down like a club on something in the flowers. Benjamin sprang from among the hollyhocks and streaked toward the back door.

Julian ran outside. "Are you crazy?" he shouted at them. "You might have killed that cat. Now get the hell out of here and stay out."

"He's a killer, that cat is. He kills," the red-haired boy said.

"I told you to get out of here. Now get."

The gang of boys moved to the wall and slowly climbed over it, looking behind them all the while, whispering to one another.

Julian, still trembling with rage, was taking ice from the tray when the first pear hit the house. He thought perhaps it fell from the tree. But then there was a volley of pears. One splattered against the glass doors of the sunroom where Anne was sitting. The doors rattled but did not break.

"Julian, you'd better do something," Anne said softly.

He dashed through the back door and was immediately hit by a pear. "Hey," he shouted, "hey, you kids, cut it out." Sticks began coming over the wall, followed by rocks and empty tin cans. And then there was the shattering of glass as a stone went through the bedroom window, and a tinkling sound as fragments of the windowpane fell to the stone steps outside the sunroom.

Julian rushed through the house, out the front door, and around to the other side of the garden wall, where he caught the boys still laughing and screaming and throwing things.

"All right, you little bastards. What the hell do you think you're doing?"

"We're only playing," someone said.

"Took a pear or two."

"Didn't do nothing, actually."

"You. What's your name?" Julian grabbed the shoulder of the tall boy who had so completely charmed him a short while earlier.

"David."

"David what?"

"I didn't do anything. It was Hughey tried to get the cat." He pointed to Hughey, the fat boy with red hair.

"Answer me. I said David what?"

"Agnatelli."

"All right, David Agnatelli, you take me straight to your father."

The boys fell silent at this and Julian moved in for the kill.

"Do you know what I am?" he said, addressing the court. "I'm a lawyer. What you call a barrister. Do you know what that means?"

They knew it meant trouble.

"Now you take me straight to your father."

"He's not in. He won't be in for another hour."

Oh God, Julian thought, now what do I do? "I'll see him in an hour. I have your name." And then inspiration struck him. "Meanwhile, you've got a clean-up job to do. You, you, and you. Climb over that wall and pick up every last scrap of rubbish you threw there."

"But we didn't do nothing," Hughey said.

"Not you. I don't want you in that yard at all. Understand? But you, you, and you. Now!"

He watched with relief as they obediently climbed the wall. "I'll take care of you later," he said to Hughey and walked away, trying to look dignified.

Anne met him at the front door.

"They're cleaning the place up," she said. "I can't believe it."

"They'd better," he said, striding straight through the house to the garden. "I'm really surprised at you," he said to David. "I thought you were much nicer boys than that," and he went on and on about what he had expected of them and how there was never an excuse for deliberate cruelty and about the damage they had done to someone else's property. By the time they finished cleaning up, Julian had thoroughly intimidated them, and he came into the house feeling a little proud of himself and a little foolish for feeling proud.

"My brave man," Anne said, and the words hung between them like an accusation.

"Well, I had to," he said after a moment, feeling only foolish now. "For the cat."

"I know you did," she said. "I know."

Late that night as they lay in bed, Julian nuzzled her cheek and shoulder and finally whispered, half confession, half apology, "I felt like such a fool trying to bully a bunch of kids as if I were the warden of a reform school."

"I know," she said, "but you had to. It was out of control. They might have killed poor Benjy." Automatically, despite her resolution, she put her hand on his stomach and moved it tentatively to his hip. She could feel the resistance and withdrew her hand.

"I'm going to read for a while," he said, and got out of bed.

"Whatever you want," she said, and lay staring at the ceiling. She pretended to be asleep when he came to bed an hour later.

At five in the morning Julian sat up in bed, wide awake after four hours' sleep. His pulse was beating heavily in his throat and something was twitching in his legs. He wanted to kick, to run. There was no more sleep for him this morning.

In the kitchen he took a tranquilizer and checked the garden for further signs of damage. The boys had not come back and, except for some trampled flowers where they had cornered Benjamin, the garden looked pretty much as the Hills had left it. He made a mental note to write them an explanation of what had happened—the torn branches, the trampled flowers, the cat. As if on cue, Benjamin poked his head out of the hollyhocks. He was stalking something. Pretending to hunt, Julian thought, seeing again the enormous pigeons and the absurd cat. He shook his head.

He put a pot of coffee on the stove. It was a beautiful morning, still a little cool, but with a strong sun, which meant perfect walking weather. He stretched, bent over to touch his toes. Well, it wasn't all bad being up early for once. Though he was barefoot, he opened the back door and stepped outside. The grass was wet.

"Hey, cat!" he called, but Benjamin at the end of the garden paid no attention. Benjamin stood crouched, head pulled in, one paw slightly raised. "Benjy!" Julian called again. The cat continued to crouch, patient, motionless. And then, so swiftly that Julian wasn't sure he saw it, Benjamin sprang at something, flailing with his paw, and then leaping back as if he were afraid. Julian frowned and began to cross the garden to see what Benjamin was hunting, but the grass was long and wet and his feet began to feel cold. "To hell with it," he said and turned back. He was pouring coffee when Benjamin came through the cat port and took up his stance at the refrigerator.

"Well, how's the old hunter?" Julian said, kneeling to pet the cat. He knew Benjamin endured the petting for the sake of the food, and he took advantage of the cat's hunger to get in several more strokes. "Nice old Benjy. Catch a pigeon, Benj? Hmmm? Hmmm?"

Benjamin meowed and rubbed his head against Julian's ankle.

"Bought love is better than none, Benj." Julian spooned a quarter tin of Sainsbury's into the blue plate; Anne could give him the rest later.

Julian was beginning to feel good. He cut two slices of bread, threw the stale one in the garbage, and spread butter thickly on the other. He hummed as he moved around the kitchen. "I'm going to invest in life," he said to the cat. "I'm going to bask in the sun with English bread and butter. That's what I have to do, and I'm going to do it. What do you think of that, fat Benjamin?"

The cat meowed for more food.

"Not on your life."

Benjamin waited until Julian went into the sunroom, and then he gave up and went back to the garden to hunt.

Julian was sitting in the wicker chair with his second cup of coffee when he spotted the toad under the bench. Good God, he thought, if I'd sat at the bench I'd have stepped on that thing barefoot. He got up and looked at it. Why on earth would anybody want to buy kids a rubber toad, he wondered. It was a perfect replica, actually. Too perfect to be real. Perhaps one of the kids bought it himself, to scare somebody. The thought crossed his mind that he was afraid to touch it, but that was silly.

He made breakfast for Anne and went upstairs to wake her. He kissed her, and then they wrestled in the bed. He thought of making love and to hell with breakfast. He would let her decide.

"I made your breakfast. It's all ready. What do you say?" And Anne, recalling his rejecting her only hours before, said, "Yummy, yummy," and slipped out of bed.

They were carrying plates of eggs and bacon into the sunroom when Julian said, "Oh, don't be scared of the rubber toad underneath your bench. The cat must have been playing with it."

Anne looked at it for a moment. "It looks real," she said, stooping to pick it up. "Yuck, it is real," and she pulled her hand away.

"It can't be real. It's too perfect. Look at the way the legs go out."

"Legs or no legs, that damned thing is real," Anne said. "The cat must have brought it in."

Julian was on his knees examining the toad. Sweat broke out on his forehead, and he could feel the pulse in his throat accelerate. His whole body went clammy.

"I'd better throw it out," he said, standing. Anne turned to look at him, surprised by the new tone in his voice.

"I'll throw it out, if you want."

"No. No, I'll do it."

Julian looked around for something he could use to pick up the toad. He found a green plastic dagger and flipped the dried-out body of the toad onto a piece of cardboard. His hands shook so badly that the toad fell off, and he had to scoop it up once more. He threw it into the bushes outside the sunroom.

"God, I hate dead things," he said. "Look, I've got goosebumps all over my arm."

"Don't think about it," Anne said. "You should just do what you have to and don't think about it." She reached for his hand and shook it back and forth. "Eat your breakfast, silly."

But Julian had lost his appetite. All that day he was quiet and moody. When he spoke, it was to ask Anne how she thought the cat had brought the toad inside, or why, or why not until now. They went to *The School for Scandal* in the evening, an awful production, Julian said, in which Lady Sneerwell was made up to look exactly like a frog. He sat up late drinking and slept only fitfully.

At sunrise he was wide awake again, his pulse racing, his legs straining to kick or run. He got up and went slowly downstairs to the kitchen. He looked around, prepared to find another dead toad, but there was nothing. He glanced into the sunroom and that too looked safe. In the garden Benjamin was curled up on the potting bench taking the sun. Julian sighed heavily and then smiled at himself. No toads. He felt as if a heavy rock had just been taken off his chest. He went about making coffee.

"I'm on the brink, Benjy," he said, spooning out the cat food. "My celebrated mind is hanging by a thread. It's full of snakes and hoppytoads and death, death, death." He stroked the cat, who only continued to eat, and then he took his coffee into the sunroom and sat on a bench facing the glass doors. Immediately he saw the toad next to the wicker chair.

"Oh God, Benjy, not another one."

Benjamin came from the kitchen and went straight to the toad. He crouched, crept up, and then nudged it tentatively with one paw.

"Get away, Benj." Julian pulled the cat away, but Benjamin returned immediately, sniffing at the toad. Julian could see blood on the carpet, and there was blood on the toad too. "Come on, Benjamin, get away!" and he struck the cat lightly on the nose. He began to feel sick to his stomach. Saliva was running in his mouth. He wanted to spit. He found the plastic dagger and prodded the toad onto a magazine; as he did so the toad kicked out one leg in a kind of dying reflex, and a large, glassy eye moved in its head. Julian dropped the dagger and the magazine and ran to the kitchen, where he threw up in the sink. He let the water run while he stood leaning against the sinkboard, staring out the window. After a while he washed out his mouth and, resolute, went back to the sunroom where quickly, almost cruelly, he pushed the toad onto the magazine and threw it into the bushes behind the potting bench. He was covered with sweat when finished. It was hideous, this half death. He saw again the eye move in the head, the leg kick out.

He sat at the table with a fresh cup of coffee. He had to get hold of himself. This was ridiculous. He wasn't afraid of toads. It was just that he had had no sleep in too long a time. It was just that he wanted to make love to Anne and, somehow, couldn't. It was just that . . . Benjamin appeared outside the doors, crouched on the potting bench, then sprang into the bushes, cried, thrashed about, and in a moment reappeared with a toad dangling from his mouth. Julian began to feel nauseous again. Slowly he twisted the key to open the glass doors and clapped his hands at the cat, who turned and looked at him and then turned away. "Drop that, Benjamin! Drop it." He picked up a newspaper and slapped it against his thigh. Benjamin got a firmer grip on the toad and disappeared into the bushes. Julian closed the doors and leaned against them. "I'll kill that damned cat," he said.

. He wandered from the sunroom to the living room and then out to the entrance hall, where there were some paperback books on a little table. He took one, Sitwell's *English Eccentrics*, and went into the kitchen and then into the sunroom, completing the circle. But from the sunroom he could see the garden, and suddenly he could not endure the sight of the garden. He took his book to the living room and sat on one of the absurdly low nursing chairs that were so uncomfortable. He sat staring at the book, not reading it. Finally he heard Anne coming down the stairs, and as he looked up from the book, he looked straight at another toad, this one much lighter in color, much larger in size.

Anne put her arms around him from behind. "My poor husband never sleeps," she said, kissing his neck. "He's going to turn into a little raccoon." She traced the dark circles beneath his eyes.

"Look," he said, pointing.

"Not another toad. Where on earth are they coming from?"

"That damned cat is where. He's out there now, in the garden, with another one hanging from his jaws. I saw him with it."

"Oh, Julian." Her voice was halfway between sympathy and exasperation.

"Well, I'd better get on with it," he said. She went to prepare breakfast while Julian once again got the plastic dagger and a magazine to scoop up the dead toad. But the toad was very much alive, and as Julian prodded and pushed, it suddenly leaped high in the air, thudding against the wall and then leaping off toward the center of the floor.

Anne rushed to the room when she heard Julian scream. He was standing with his back to the wall, his eyes horribly dilated, his face bloodless.

"I can't stand it," he said. "I've got to get out of here. I've got to get out of this house. The place is alive with frogs. I can feel them all over me and that cat, that vicious cat, keeps bringing them in. More of them."

She looked at him, a complete stranger to her. "Get out," she said. "Go into the kitchen. Julian, do you hear me? Go into the kitchen and close both doors. I'll get rid of it."

"I've got to," he said. "I've got to do it. I'm the man."

"Do what I said."

Trembling, white, Julian went into the kitchen. He looked out the back door and, as he expected, there was a dead toad on the step. Outside the sunroom he could see Benjamin hunting among the hollyhocks. There was another dead toad on the potting bench.

He sat at the table and covered his face with his hands.

Afterward Anne convinced him they could not move to a hotel since the Hills would not be returning for another two days. She insisted she could manage the cat. She would block off the cat port, keeping Benjamin outside the house during the day and inside at night. That way there would never be a time when he came in unobserved. Nearly desperate, Julian agreed to this.

That night, near midnight, they were lying in bed reading when they heard a racket downstairs in the kitchen.

"Somebody at the door," Anne said.

"No. It's that damned cat trying to get out." Anne had propped a carving board against the cat port but Julian, not taking any chances, had further fortified the board by placing a heavy chair against it.

In a few minutes they heard Benjamin scrambling up the stairs. He stood outside their open door and meowed. It was not the sound he made for food or for attention; it was a different sound altogether.

"Poor cat. She's lonely," Anne said.

"Poor cat, my ass. That damned thing is evil. Look, he's coming to get you."

Benjamin moved across the carpet and then bounded onto the foot of the huge bed.

"Poor sweet Benjy," Anne said.

Benjamin made no move to curl up. Instead, slinking, he moved slowly toward the head of the bed, his claws sinking through the woolen blanket into Anne's thighs and stomach. He crouched for a moment and then moved up to her breast.

"See," Julian said, "he *is* after you," and as he said it, joking, the cat suddenly ducked its head and hissed. With one swift movement Julian got his hands under the cat's front feet and lifted him high above the bed and then onto the floor. Benjamin sprang for the door and hid somewhere on the darkened stairs.

"My God, did you know?" Anne said.

"No, I was fooling. What do you make of that?"

"Maybe she was playing. It didn't look like playing."

"I think she's crazy. *He's* crazy. I think he turns into a predator at night."

"No. Not really."

"No wonder they associate cats with witches. With the devil."

"Poor Benj. You know, she scared me half to death? Could I have a drink, Ju? I mean, would you mind going down and getting it?"

"Sure. Man versus cat. Man versus forces of evil. Have no fear, m'dear, Julian is here." He laughed, trembling.

He threw on the lights for the stairs and started down. Benjamin appeared from behind him and raced ahead into the kitchen, where he began clawing at the chair blocking the cat port. Julian went to the refrigerator for ice, but for once the cat didn't want food. He wanted only to get out. Julian glanced at him as he made the drinks. Benjamin was different, there was no doubt. For a long minute Julian stared at him and the cat stared back. It was as if they both knew something and neither dared say it.

"Okay, cat, time's up," he said, and lifted him out of the kitchen into the hall. At once the cat wriggled free and returned to scratching at the chair that blocked the door. Frightened, furious, Julian pounced on him. "I said no." Holding the cat in his outstretched hands, he walked down the hall and threw him, with rather more force than he had intended, into the living room. The cat set up a furious screeching and began to tear at the carpet. Julian closed the kitchen doors both to the sunroom and to the hall and took the drinks and went upstairs. On the upper landing he turned and looked down at a sharp angle into the living room, where he could see two gray eyes burning in the darkness. He shivered, knowing what he had to do.

The next night before bed, Anne packed their bags and tidied the house. She wanted things to look neat for the cleaning woman.

"It's been a strange vacation, hasn't it," she said. "First the sickness, then the Walpurgisnacht kids, and then the cat with all those frogs."

"I hate that cat."

"Poor Benjy. You know, I wonder if we'll ever come back here again."

"I have no desire to. You?"

"Not really. Something's different now. Spoiled." She was tucking makeup things into a silk traveling purse. "Julian? Can we make love soon? When we get home?"

"Of course. Maybe before we get home."

"Well, no. Home is all right. But we need it, you know?"

"Yes, I know."

When it was time for bed, he said to her, "You sleep. I'm going to read downstairs for a while. In fact, I'll let the cat out and block the door."

"Will she be all right outside? What if it rains?"

"It's not going to rain. And then we won't have to worry about him going crazy in the house again."

"Okay."

He kissed her. "And then maybe in the morning we'll get them old colored lights going. A little farewell gesture to Merrie England."

"I just want you your old self."

"I am, nearly. I've decided I'm going to invest in life. I'm going to join the human race."

"My sweet Julian," she said.

"You sleep now," he said, and kissed her again.

Downstairs he poured himself a drink and waited. Benjamin ignored him at first, stalking from room to room, his head stretched forward, his tail erect and swaying. And then after a while he began to claw at the door. Julian thrust him roughly aside and the cat hissed. Deliberately taking his time, he poured himself another drink, sipped it, and only then moved the chair and the carving board away from the door. At once the cat sprang through the little opening. Julian opened the door wide and stepped outside. There was a quarter moon and clouds drifting across it. He inhaled deeply; a beautiful night; a perfect night. He heard the cat hunting in the bushes.

He found the red clay flower pot he was looking for and brought it into the house. It was so heavy he had trouble carrying it; the earth inside had hardened almost to cement. He set it down in the sunroom next to the glass doors. He unlocked the doors and stood looking into the garden for several minutes.

Julian was sitting at the table composing a long note to the Hills when he looked up and saw Benjamin slink from the steps to the stone slab that served as a potting bench. He put down the pen.

He had just explained to the Hills that there had been trouble with the gang of boys next door, that they had stolen pears and broken branches and trampled flowers. He explained how they had repeatedly tormented the cat, how they had tried to beat him with sticks and pelt him with stones. He hoped the Hills would do something to insure poor Benjamin's safety.

It was then that he put down his pen, seeing Benjamin outside the doors. He waited for a moment and, as he expected, Benjamin disappeared into the bushes and reappeared after a while, a toad hanging from his mouth, kicking, but firmly hooked in those thin, pointed fangs. Julian moved to the doors, opened them, and stood watching Benjamin release the toad, poke it until it tried to hop away, and then swipe it with a swift paw, sinking his fangs into it once more. Julian watched this until at last the toad could make no more movements at all. Benjamin gave it a few more pokes, but when the toad failed to respond, he turned from it and assumed a totally different posture. His body seemed to inflate, and he arched his back while his fur stood stiff from his neck to his tail. And then he crouched, his belly flattened against the stone slab, his whole attention directed to something moving in the bushes. He inched forward, his claws still tucked in, but his head already arched in its hunting position, his fangs bared.

Julian lifted the heavy flower pot high in the air and brought it heavily, with both hands, down on the cat's head. The body convulsed and lay still. There was no sound. When he tipped the pot away with his foot, Julian discovered the head mashed flat. He stared at the bloody pulp and was relieved to feel nothing. Calmly, methodically, he picked up the cat by a hind foot and carried it across the garden to the compost heap. He kicked a small pile of weeds over the body. He returned to the potting bench, where he picked the dead frog up in his hand and threw it into the bushes. Then he tipped the hardened earth out of the pot onto the bloodied places where bits of the cat's fur still clung. He left the empty clay pot next to the potting bench.

Inside, he washed his hands and poured himself another drink. He was perfectly calm, perfectly in control. He sat down and finished the note to the Hills, hoping they had had a pleasant holiday and promising to return next year with Anne so that they might enjoy the delights of London, but especially so they might visit the beloved Benjamin.

Julian signed the note, placed the carving board and the chair against the cat port, and then went slowly, happily up the stairs. In the bedroom he would wake Anne. It had been a long night, a long vacation, and he was ready now, eager for mad, desperate love.

A FAMILY AFFAIR

1

IN THAT country there was never a wind. Sun beat down from
April to October, and the fields that surrounded the town grew
pale yellow and then dark yellow and then brown. There was no
green anywhere.

Dust hung in the air, flung by the wheels of jeeps as the soldiers tore down Finial Street to the Blue Spider Cafe. Cozy Oaks
was also located on Finial Street; in fact, it was separated from
the Blue Spider only by Adam's Bakery and Johnson's Wood and
Hardware, but the soldiers never went to Cozy Oaks. The men
from the farms went there, and the men from the foundry, but
the soldiers went to the Blue Spider.

All during February and March they sang around the jukebox,
and the sound drifted slowly past Adam's and Johnson's until the
regulars at Cozy Oaks would shake their heads and shrug their
shoulders, but nobody ever complained because, one way or
another, everyone was a little better off since the soldiers had
come. In April, with all the windows open, the singing and the
short high whoops that meant they were having a good time could
be heard far out in the fields and sometimes even beyond that,
in the pocked desert where the base was located and where the
lucky soldiers with cars brought the girls from the Spider who
would go all the way.

It had been like this every spring of the past four years, even
when the base was new and nobody had yet sorted out how they

really felt about the soldiers. Beryl Gerriter gave birth that first spring to her son Jason, her deep moans and howls punctuated with the drunken singing from the Blue Spider. Luke Gerriter waited in the sitting room with his daughter Elissa. They said nothing, though from time to time he would send her to the kitchen to get him another beer.

"Why can't I go in?" she asked him.

"Shut your mouth. You're not old enough."

"Twelve is old enough."

He held his beer can to his mouth for a long slug and then he looked at her. Nothing. A face like an axe, everything pulled out to a point, with her mouth pinched already like Beryl's, a worried face. And skinny. How in hell would he ever marry her off?

"Twelve isn't old enough for much," he said.

She knew his voice when he spoke like that, she was afraid of it, she didn't know why. She leaned over Pal and hugged him, rubbing the fur along his back.

"We should get rid of that mutt. It stinks. That's what the hell's the matter around here. That mutt. One of these days I'm going to take him out and shoot him."

She said nothing. He was just drinking; his threats didn't mean anything.

Voices drifted in from the Blue Spider. They were singing "Poor Lil." In the other room Beryl smiled sourly at the idea of poor Lil. Poor Berla, she thought, and she pushed again. By Christ, she'd never have another baby. She could feel her skin tear, she was being ripped apart. Someone mopped her forehead, someone pressed at her thighs. And that bastard in the other room, getting drunk, it was his fault. Oh God! She pushed again. There was a huge surge between her legs, and for a moment she went unconscious. She woke screaming.

Outside the room Luke waited out the scream and then slammed his beer can to the floor in fury. "If she don't hurry up in there! Hurry up, you!" he shouted at the bedroom door. "I said, hurry up!"

The bedroom door opened and Dr. Pharon stuck his head out. "We've got problems," he said, "serious ones. It's gonna be a while, and I can't promise anything. But I suggest, if you got a brain left in that addled head of yours, that you stop drinking and start praying and, whatever else you do, you shut up." And he closed the door.

"I'll be at the Oaks," Luke said to his daughter. "You can come and get me when the mule is born."

Elissa nodded, her eyes glazed with fear, and she hugged Pal again. "It's going to be all right, Pal," she said, rocking back and forth, the dog's muzzle in her lap. "Everything's going to be all right. Everything."

She was awakened later by Dr. Pharon, who told her to go find her father; he had something important to tell him.

Outside she paused for a minute to think what she was doing. She did so many things automatically that sometimes she had to stop and tell herself what came next. She had trouble catching her breath; the sun had gone down, but there was no breeze. In the distance she could hear loud shouts and singing. She tried again to catch her breath, and in the still air she could taste the dust. She crossed the lawn to the evergreen tree and held a spiky branch to her face, breathing its sharp smell of oil and gum, a bitter smell, but special to her. The tree was yellow, almost green, and with her face buried in its branches she could forget the damp heat and the taste of dust.

Pal whimpered at her feet.

"It's all right," she said, and ran down the dirt road to where it met Finial Street. A small stone caught in the sole of her sneaker, and she stooped under the streetlight to poke it out. It had wedged between the rubber sole and the canvas lining, and the more she pried at the hole the deeper she pushed the stone.

A jeep roared by, throwing dust in her eyes and hair.

"Damn," she said, "damn it."

And then the jeep screeched to a halt and backed up, crookedly, weaving from side to side.

"Hi there, sweetheart."

"She's too young, Ron."

"They're never too young."

Elissa stared at them, not frightened. They were soldiers from the base. Nobody minded the soldiers. The men had jobs now that the soldiers had come. Even her father had a job.

"What do you say, sweetheart? You want a ride?"

He was blond, with a wide funny smile. He was the most beautiful man she had ever seen.

"I've got to go to the Oaks to get my father."

"Well, you jump right in here between me and my friend and we'll take you straight to the Oaks." He leaped out and held the low door open. She hesitated.

"Come on. You'll be all right."

"For Christ sake, Ron," the driver said.

"What about my dog?"

"Bring your dog too. Come on."

She climbed into the jeep and held out her arms for Pal, who wriggled from the soldier's hands into her lap. Ron climbed in beside her, slamming the small door. "And away we go," he shouted as the jeep took off. His arm, thrown over the seat at her back, drifted gradually to her shoulder. She could feel his hand lightly touching her bare arm.

"What's your name, sweetheart?"

"Elissa," she said, throwing her head back to feel the air blowing in her face.

"Elissa. Well, that's some name. I never heard of a name like Elissa. I think I'd call you Cookie, 'cause you're so sweet." He put his hand on her knee and ran it slowly up toward her thigh.

"Ron, if you want to get your ass in jail, you're going in just the right direction," the driver said.

"What's the matter, for Christ sake? I'm only petting the dog." The two men in back laughed. Ron rubbed Pal's ears and his back. "Isn't that right, Cookie? No harm in petting the nice little doggie."

Elissa thought she had never been so happy.

"My mother just had a baby," she said. "I've got to tell my father."

"That right?" Ron said, his hand going back to her thigh. "You gonna have a baby? Hmmm? Would you like a baby?"

His hand was hot on her thin dress and she could feel sweat break out on her thigh and up higher. She wished he would move his hand there. She wanted him to touch her all over. But most of all she wanted to put her two arms around his neck and lay her head on his chest and just stay like that for a long, long time.

"Cozy Oaks," the driver said, slamming on the brakes.

And then she was out of the jeep and it was roaring off, the men in back laughing and Ron shouting, "See you around, Cookie." She stood for a long while watching the trail of dust the jeep left behind. She could still feel each of his fingers on her thigh and his thumb moving back and forth.

All the way home she repeated their conversation in her mind. I think I'd call you Cookie, 'cause you're so sweet, he had said. And he had asked if she would like a baby. She put her hand on her thigh where he had put his. For once she did not care that her father was stumbling along in the dark, cursing every goddamn stone in his path, the goddamn wife who called him away from his buddies, the goddamn baby that would put them all in the poorhouse. She had not even minded going into Cozy Oaks to get him. She had only half heard the sarcastic comments of the men at the bar, the double-meaning jokes, the laughter. While he bought a round of beer for everyone, she had stood at the screen door looking down toward the Blue Spider, where Ron was probably dancing or drinking with some pretty girl he was calling Cookie because she was so sweet, but it didn't matter. He had been nice, and whether he meant it or not, he had said it.

"You said it's a boy."

"What?" She stopped and tried to wiggle the stone into another part of her shoe.

"The baby. You said it's a boy."

"Yes."

"Did you see it?"

"No. Dr. Pharon said to go right away."

"Then how do you know it's a boy?" His voice was angry.

"I don't know. I just think it is. I don't know."

She put her arm up to ward off the blow, but he had only meant to caress her. They stood looking at one another.

"I thought you were going to hit me."

"I never hit you. You're like your mother, you try to put me in the wrong. You try to make me look bad."

"No. I don't. I . . ." She lowered her eyes.

He put his arm around her shoulder now, stiffly, feeling the small tense muscles beneath his fingers. They walked this way, father and child in a book of photographs, until they reached the little house where all the lights were on.

Dr. Pharon explained patiently that Beryl had had a breech birth and, though there was not necessarily a connection, the child was a mongoloid and would probably not live long. The mother had required many stitches, she was seriously ill. She should be in a hospital, but there was no hospital, and so he would have to pay Mrs. Botts to stay with her.

Luke Gerriter listened with his head in his hands, and when the doctor left, he saw him to the door. Then he went into the bedroom, where he looked in the crib for a long moment, for the last time. He stared at the gray figure in the bed.

"So you had to do this to me, too," he said. "One lay in three years, and you had to produce this. You bitch." He turned at the door to look at her again. "You miserable bitch," he said, and lumbered up the stairs to Elissa's attic room.

Elissa stretched out on the sitting room couch where she stroked Pal and whispered over and over again, "It's all right; it's going to be all right."

2

The next morning Luke bought a bed frame that folded in half and a mattress to go with it, and he set them up in the tiny bedroom. He said nothing to Beryl—everything between them seemed to have been said already—and she remained with her face turned resolutely to the wall. She had not asked to see the baby.

With the double bed taking up most of the room and then with the dresser and the baby's crib, Mrs. Botts found she had no place for the chair she had brought in from the kitchen. So she perched on the edge of Luke's folding bed, knitting, talking to herself, and at regular intervals feeding the baby. This sort of thing had happened before; the answer was to wait. The little thing would die eventually or, if he lived and grew up, they'd adjust. People always did. She moved closer to the window hoping to catch a breath of air, though she knew there was never a breeze here. Elissa would be along soon to relieve her.

Almost at once they had settled into a regular routine. At three o'clock Elissa returned from school and Mrs. Botts went home. Elissa prepared her father's dinner and then he disappeared until midnight or later, when he came stumbling home from the Oaks. Meanwhile Elissa sat with her mother, saying nothing. No one in the house said anything.

Elissa had instructions from Mrs. Botts about caring for the baby, and she went about the work methodically, automatically; it was the way she made dinner, the way she did schoolwork; it was as if there were some more important part of her that simply stepped out and walked away, leaving the methodical, automatic Elissa behind to do the work.

School was the worst part of the day. The others teased her about her idiot brother, and once one of the teachers had called her aside in the schoolyard and asked about her mother and her father and finally about her brother. She wanted to know if he had a big head and if his eyes were pink; she asked her to describe him. Elissa said she didn't know how and tried to pull away, but the teacher had hold of her arm.

"You tell me, you hear. I've got to know these things. I'm only doing my duty." She tightened her grasp on the girl's arm.

Elissa tried to run, but could not get away. And then something inside her took over, and it was as if she were talking with her father when he was drunk and impossible. She said in her dreamy way, "He's just a baby, just a little ordinary baby. His eyes are blue, a pretty light blue they are, and his head is only as big as a baby's head. He cries when he's hungry and then my mother feeds him, but most of the time he just laughs and plays with his toys and sleeps. Just like any baby."

"Are you telling me the truth?"

"Yes, ma'am."

"That isn't what everybody says. What do you say to that?"

"Maybe they haven't seen him," Elissa said. "He's a real nice baby."

More and more she found herself alone; she played with the dog and sat with the baby in her mother's room, waiting.

Luke found himself more and more in the center of things. Somebody was always standing him a beer at the Oaks, and the men went out of their way not to mention births or babies. Work was going well, too, with a good raise following the birth of the child and the foreman keeping out of his way at the foundry. It was only at home that life was impossible. He had to be very drunk before he could get courage to come back to that small bedroom smelling of sour sheets and milk and lie there knowing Beryl was not asleep and that thing lay in the darkness between them.

He thought sometimes he would get up and place a pillow over the baby's face and put it out of its misery. He thought of shooting it. Some nights as he turned off Finial Street into the dirt road that led to his house, he saw himself approach the door and walk through the house and down the cellar stairs and get a gun—the small pistol maybe, with its shiny blue barrel, or one of the rifles —and go back up the stairs, through the sitting room and into the bedroom, and there . . . He could not imagine the rest in detail, but there was one small shot into the crib and then a scream from Beryl, followed by two shots and then a silence. He held the gun at his own head. On those dark nights staggering home from Finial Street, he would weep at how rotten life was, how wrong everything had turned out. He would go home and fall into bed, and it did not matter any more that Beryl was lying there awake, staring straight ahead.

Beryl seemed to be awake all the time. She lay in bed motionless, turning from side to side only when she had to be washed or when Mrs. Botts changed the sheets. She ate whatever they brought her, and when they asked if she wanted more, she shook her head no.

After the first day Mrs. Botts gave up trying to talk to Beryl but she could never be sure whether Beryl was asleep or awake. Sometimes it was as if she were staring even when her eyes were shut. She'd be plumb glad, she told herself, when this whole thing was over.

Only Elissa was indifferent to Beryl's silent stare. Often, coming home from school, she would stand at the bedroom door and look at her mother, thinking, she'll never come back, she's gotten away to some place where there are trees and air and no more shouting and she'll never come back. She envied her.

And Beryl lay there, with her gray face on the pillow, staring. It was almost a month before she asked to see the baby. There had been no warning, no signs of a return to life; suddenly one afternoon she simply turned in the bed, lifted herself on one elbow, and spoke to Mrs. Botts. Her voice was clear and strong.

"Let me see it," she said.

Mrs. Botts looked up from her knitting. "How's that?"

"Let me see it. The baby."

"Well, now, Berla. Are you real sure you want to do that? Might be as how well enough should be let alone till you're feeling better."

"I'm real sure."

Mrs. Botts picked up the baby and laid him in the bed next to Beryl, who twisted beneath the sheet so that she could get a better look at him. She took a long deep breath, and her chest heaved twice, as if she were going to sob. And then she whispered "No," a breathy sound that turned into a deep moan. She picked up the baby and crushed it to her breast, bending from the waist and swaying her body from side to side as she clutched the white, unresisting thing.

Mrs. Botts stroked Beryl's hair and said over and over, "That's all right, Berla, you go ahead and cry. That's all right, Berla," and she went on stroking, waiting for the release of tears. But the tears did not come. Beryl stopped moaning and released the baby. She placed it on her lap and forced herself into a sitting position.

After a long while she said, "Look at it. Just look at it."

The baby had smooth, almost puffy skin, moist in the airless room. His ears were small and round, and his nose only a blob of flesh, not like a nose at all. His lips were thick, the color of raw meat. Beryl bent closer and looked at his tongue. It had two deep grooves and protruded from his tiny mouth. But it was his head that astonished her most. It was small and hard and completely round. She had expected something huge, a monstrosity, an enormous watermelon head. Looking at him at first, she had been relieved, she had almost begun to hope. And then she recalled the doctor's warning. "He's a mongoloid, he will never be normal, he will probably not live very many years," and she saw the huge lips and the tiny slits for eyes. With her thumb she gently pushed up one eyelid. The eye was milky blue and empty.

She had not wanted him, she had not wanted sex in the first place, and now this had happened. She crooked her finger under his tiny palm and looked at his hand. Even his hands were wrong. There was a space between his first finger and the rest. His feet had that same strange cleft, as if they were paws, as if he were Pal.

"Put him back," she said, and then a long while later, "I'm going to call him Jason." Her mouth bent in a thin, bitter smile.

She was herself again for a few months, and then in the fall she had a hysterectomy, and after that she left the baby's care entirely to Elissa. She never wanted to see him again, she said.

Jason died just before his second birthday.

3

Elissa missed him. He was not a mongoloid to her, some strange monster her father would not look at, or a mockery her mother hated. He was that ordinary little baby she had told her teacher about, a baby who cried when he was hungry, but who most of the time played with his toys and slept. She was able to feed him, change him, and never see anything but that ordinary baby. Ron's baby, she liked to think, or the baby of somebody, anybody, who loved her. She would have a baby of her own someday, in a place different from this one; and she would be loved someday too.

Elissa was fourteen now and plain. Her hair was long and thin, falling straight on either side of her wedge-shaped face. She looked nearsighted, though she was not. The glassy look in her eyes came from daydreaming, her teachers said, but Elissa knew it was something different from daydreaming. She was escaping, she was going away.

With Jason dead, no one teased her at school any more. Among the other girls there was even some grudging admiration of her breasts, which were rounder and fuller than their own. They could tell she didn't use cotton either, as most of them did. But she was plain, she was no threat to them. They merely laughed indifferently when she was called on in class and admitted she hadn't heard the question. The boys ignored her altogether, except to joke about her breasts as they passed in the corridor. "Maybe with a bag over her head," they would say, cupping their hands in front of their chests. Elissa was oblivious. School would be over if you waited long enough.

Soon after Jason died, she had begun taking Pal for walks each evening. After supper, when her father left for the Oaks and her mother settled into her chair by the radio, Elissa took the dog and walked slowly down the dirt road to Finial Street. She pulled a stick of straw grass from a clump by the road and chewed on it, kicking stones ahead for Pal to chase. She walked slower as she came into sight of Finial Street, and under the streetlight she stopped and waited. When she heard one of the jeeps approach she bent over as if she were taking a stone from her shoe. She liked the feeling of the blood racing to her temple, the hammering in her chest. This was how she had met Ron. It could happen again.

And then one night a jeep did stop and come roaring back.

"Hi," a girl said, giggling. She was in the front seat beside a soldier, and there were two other soldiers in the back. Her dark red hair tumbled around her shoulders in big curls and her mouth glistened with lipstick. It took Elissa a full minute to recognize her as Florence Kath. Florence was also a freshman at the high school.

"Hi," Elissa said, her eyes darting from face to face. Ron was not there. "Oh, it's you. I didn't recognize you, you're so . . ."

"We're going to the Spider," Florence said. "Want to come?"

"Yeah, why don't you come?" a soldier in back said. "Here, you can sit right between us. We'll take care of you." The other just grinned.

"I'd like to," she said. "I really would, but my dog . . . I've got to get back home." She could not take her eyes off the soldier in front who had his arm around Florence and was pushing the shoulder of her peasant blouse lower and lower.

"Fresh bastard," Florence said, pleased, and she pushed his hand away. "Come on, Lissa, you'll really love it."

"I can't," she said, "I just can't. My father . . ." She stood there speechless as the jeep took off, scattering dust everywhere.

Elissa and Florence became friends. Each morning during third period they met in the girls' room and smoked a cigarette. And they ate lunch together. Though they ate in the cafeteria with everyone else, there were always empty chairs at their table. Florence was cheap, everyone said; Florence did it with the soldiers.

"You ought to come to the Spider, Lissa, it's really terrific. I go only on Saturdays now, but next year I'm gonna go on Fridays and Saturdays too, once I convince my old lady. You ought to come."

"My mother would never let me."

"Well, you ought to come anyway. Last Saturday there was this guy. Oh my God, he was so cute. He bought me a beer by buying it for himself, you know, and letting me drink it. He had real curly hair, black, and we necked like crazy right in the booth. I didn't care. And when he took me home, woo, woo."

"What happened when he took you home?"

Florence sang, "But I ain't gonna tell you what he did to me." She sang loudly so the kids at the next table would hear her. "I don't care about them bastards," she said. "I don't care about any of them. They all ought to go get laid."

"What happened when he took you home? Tell me."

"Nosey bitch, aren't you. I'll tell you on Saturday when we put up our hair."

Every Saturday morning they put up their hair in huge pink rollers, whispering and giggling at the kitchen sink, splashing water everywhere. Then they sat outside on the back steps letting the sun dry their hair.

Beryl would sometimes come out, not actually joining them, just leaning against the doorframe smoking a cigarette. She had put on weight since her operation, and the faded housecoat she invariably wore bulged now with two small rolls around her waist. She kept her hair tied back with a blue and white bandanna.

"Boy-crazy," she would say, and the girls would giggle. "I know," she said, nodding in agreement with herself, "don't think for a minute I don't know."

And sometimes she would study the two girls. Elissa was developing a good bust. Funny about that, because she was so skinny, especially in the face. She'd get a man someday, all right. Beryl smiled bitterly to herself. Florence was pasty white, with a plump face and a red mouth that was always pouting. She's looking for trouble, Beryl thought, and she'll find it.

"You keep going to that Spider," she would say, "and you'll get what you're looking for."

And once she said, "You kids, you think you know. I was like that once. Everything looks rosy. You think getting married is going to be the greatest thing in the world. Hah!" She lit another cigarette, her face pinched in concentration. "I remember when I was a kid, about your age, maybe younger, I thought getting married was the best thing that could happen to anybody, just getting away, not having to answer to nobody for nothing. I thought men were . . ." She was looking out over their heads, squinting against the sun, and then suddenly she threw down her cigarette and ground it out. "Men," she said. "They only want one thing." She went inside and slammed the door.

Florence waited a minute until she was sure Beryl was gone and then she said, "Jesus, your mother, is she ever some kind of nut! She's worse than mine. My old lady just keeps nagging and nagging, but at least she's not crazy." She touched the rollers on top of her head. "You know something? I think she's really crazy. I really do."

"It's since the baby died," Elissa said. "And then her operation."

"Maybe it's the change. They get crazy during the change, that's what Tussie told me. Tussie's my aunt, and is she ever gorgeous. She's the one that showed me how to put on makeup and everything. She told me all about sex and everything. Woo woo. As if I didn't know already." She shrieked with laughter, and Elissa laughed with her.

Florence rummaged through the large embroidered bag she carried everywhere with her. She pulled out her makeup box, flat plastic containers of base and powder and rouge, and she gazed into a small round mirror as she drew the crimson lipstick across her mouth. She was making it larger, she explained. Men liked lips that way, it was sexy. She held the lipstick lovingly, caressing her lips with it, gently expanding her lip line above and below its natural ridges. Her lips looked wet. She pursed them at the mirror, lazily stuck her tongue out and curled it to one side of her mouth, tossed her head back, and gazed into the mirror with half-closed eyes. She was thinking of tonight, of what might happen.

Elissa looked at her and ached. The pancake makeup, the hair in rollers, the glistening red mouth. Some day she would go to the Blue Spider. Some day all that excitement would be hers.

4

On the night before her fifteenth birthday, Elissa woke to angry shouting. It was a sweltering night and she had kicked the sheet off, but now she pulled it over her and pressed the pillow against her ears. Sweat was running from her forehead into her eyes. Her head ached. She took the pillow away from her ears. They were still shouting.

She could hear her mother's voice screaming "bastard" over and over against her father's drunken laughter, a choked, hollow laugh with no joy in it. Pal was whimpering at the foot of the bed. Her mother's voice grew louder and she heard her father's voice too, thick and angry, though she could not make out what he was saying. And then there was a crash. A table must have been tipped over or something heavy thrown. The voices stopped. The house was completely silent. A floorboard creaked and Pal whimpered once again, but the house remained silent the rest of the night.

The next day Beryl and Luke did not speak to one another, nor would she sit with him while he ate. When Luke returned from work the table was set for him and Elissa, and the dinner was ready on the counter next to the stove. Beryl sat in the bedroom looking out the window. Elissa and her father ate in silence, Elissa only toying with her food. She was not hungry.

On the third day Luke said to her, "Where's your mother?"

"In the bedroom."

"Doesn't she eat at all? When does she eat?"

"She eats before you come home." Elissa pushed the beans

around her plate with her fork. "Can't this stop?" she said. "Can't this all stop?"

She held her breath, fearing what he might say or do. But he only went on eating, mopping his plate finally with a piece of bread. He leaned over the table, his head in his hands. Elissa listened to the kitchen clock ticking, saw her father shake his head from side to side. It will always be like this, she thought, nothing will ever change. She will sit in the other room looking out the window and he will sit here with his head in his hands and I will be between them listening to the clock tick and tick and tick. She wanted to run, she wanted to scream, it was better to be dead.

Luke stopped shaking his head from side to side. He looked up from his plate, his eyes strange and wild, his face bruised-looking. He was not drunk now; she had never seen him look like this.

"Oh, Christ," he said, his face contracting, growing hard. "What's the use? What's the goddamn use?"

The next day he went back to his guns. He had three of them; two were heavy-gauge shotguns and the other was a twenty-two, revolver size, with a snub barrel. He had not touched them since the soldiers came and he had gotten a regular job. But before that, in that endless time when there had been no work and he had a wife and daughter to support, he had spent the days hacking at the sand and stone that stretched for miles behind the tiny house, trying to coax the sterile land into producing vegetables. And at the end of the day, when they had eaten dinner, he would get out the guns. With Beryl and Elissa by his side he trudged to the end of the garden, where he placed tin cans on a large rock to use for target practice. He was quiet and methodical, setting up the cans and walking back to the shooting box drawn in the sand, lifting the gun to his shoulder, clicking back the safety catch, firing. Elissa watched as his face tightened in concentration, his jaw went hard as he focused on the target, and his chest expanded in a sort of sigh as the bullet struck the can and sent it spinning into the air. He did this over and over until it grew dusky, and then they went into the house. None of them enjoyed the shooting; it seemed, somehow, a necessity. He had taught Beryl to shoot the twenty-two and insisted that Elissa learn also. But all this had stopped once the soldiers came and there were jobs and money. He had not bothered since then to oil and polish the guns; weeds grew here and there in the patch that had once been the garden. They should have been happy, Elissa thought, but it had not worked out that way. And now he was back with his guns.

"What's he do that for, anyhow? What's he want to shoot tin cans for?" Florence narrowed her eyes and stared into the distance where Elissa's father was shooting. It was Saturday and they were doing their hair. "That makes me really jumpy, boy, that gunshot."

"It's just a hobby. He just does target practice."

"Jeez, your family. I'd be afraid to live here. Honest to God. With your mother in the change and everything and your old man shooting out back, I'd be afraid he'd go off his nut and shoot me. How do you know he's not gonna miss some day and hit somebody by accident? Or your dog, maybe. Where is he, anyhow? Maybe your old man shot him. Maybe he's using him for target practice."

"No, he's up in my room. He's afraid of guns. He's always been afraid of guns. The noise."

"He smells, that dog. He really does. If there's one thing I can't stand in a house, it's a smelly dog. I like everything really clean. That's why I wash all my own stuff. I like it really clean."

"Wait a minute. Shhh." Elissa stared out across the ruined garden at her father. "I think he called me," she said. He was waving his arm at her. "He must have," she said, and began walking toward him.

"Watch out he don't use you for target practice," Florence said, adding softly, "what a bunch of nuts."

Luke was standing in a litter of tin cans holding a small bunch of purple flowers. They were weeds that had somehow grown through the barren soil and bloomed now in the shade of the rock Luke set the tin cans on. The stems were thick with brownish green leaves, and the blossoms were small but numerous. "Here," he said, handing the flowers to Elissa. "Wait a minute," and he stooped to pick two more and then a third stalk. "Here, take these."

"What should I do with them?"

"Take them in to her."

"What should I say?"

Luke had turned from her and was bent over picking up cans.
"Don't say anything. Just give them to her."

"Should I say they're from you?"

"I don't care what you say. Say whatever you want. Just give
them to her. Say, yes, you can say they're from me." He was lining
up cans on the rock. He was sweating.

"I'll tell her," Elissa said.

"Oh, and kid, Elissa." He scratched his head and stared at the
ground. He spoke so softly she could hardly hear him. "Tell
me, uh, tell me what she says."

Elissa ran to the house, her heart pounding. It would end now,
the fights and the anger and the silence. She showed Florence
the flowers and then ran up the porch stairs.

"Flowers," Florence said. "Big deal. Big fat hairy deal," and she
giggled to herself. Elissa had already disappeared into the house.

Suddenly she was shy. She did not know how to give her mother
the flowers, how to say they were from her father. She went slowly
into the bedroom and stood there. Beryl was sitting with her face
to the window. Her blue and white bandanna had come loose and
the hair at the back of her head stuck out in little clumps; it was
matted and damp at the temples. She turned and blew a stream of
smoke from the corner of her mouth. Her eyes were swollen and
there were dark smudges beneath them. She looked at Elissa
questioningly and then she saw the flowers.

"What are those? What the hell have you got there?"

"Look." Elissa held out the bouquet to her.

Beryl began to tremble, her mouth working furiously and her
eyes darting from Elissa to the door behind her and then back
to the flowers.

"Where did you get those?" she said, breathless. "Are they from
him? Did he tell you to bring me those?" Her voice rose; she was
almost screaming. "Get those out of this house! Get them out of
here! Out! Get out!" She stood up, one hand at her hair.

Elissa backed to the door. "They're only flowers. He just wanted
to give you some flowers."

"Look at them. They're death flowers. Death! You put those
on coffins. Don't you see? Don't you see what he wants? He wants
to get rid of me. He wants me dead." She dropped her voice to a

whisper. She was clutching Elissa's arm, her thumb and fingernails deep in the soft flesh. "He can get rid of me, you know. He has grounds. You can get rid of a woman like me. Once you can't have children any more, once you're like a chicken with its guts ripped out, they can get rid of you. He'd like to too, that's what he wants."

"He just wanted to make up. He just wanted to give you the flowers."

Elissa pulled away from her but Beryl continued on, talking rapidly, in a whisper, her words piling furiously on one another.

"You're with him too. You're like him. The both of you, you want to drive me crazy. You want me to go crazy and then you can get rid of me. Bringing me those flowers. Death flowers." She began to scream again. "Get them out of here. Get out."

Elissa ran out of the house and stood on the back porch, white and gasping for breath. Inside she could hear her mother sobbing wildly. Florence was staring at her, motionless, one hand gently touching the pink rollers on her head, the other suspended halfway to her mouth. Somewhere in the distance her father was waiting. And all she could feel was the sun, beating heavily on her head and shoulders, numbing her entire body. There was a terrible crashing sound in her head, rhythmic and painfully loud, like a gunshot; but it was not a gunshot, it was something inside her head and it would not stop. Florence was saying something, but she could not hear it.

"Wait. Wait," she said, "it'll stop."

Florence watched her come stiffly down the stairs, walking as if she were in a trance. Her arms hung limply by her sides and the flowers in her left hand trailed along the ground as she step by step approached her father. He was standing with one foot on the rock, staring off into the space that stretched out forever behind the house. As she approached him, he turned and saw the flowers. He made a sound that was half laughter and half groan.

"She didn't want them?"

"No."

"What did she say? Did you say they were from me?"

"She said to get them out of the house."

"But did she say why?"

"She said they were death flowers. She said you wanted her dead, because . . . She said you wanted to drive her crazy, that we both did."

Luke's face went gray and he put the gun down carefully against the rock. He began walking toward the house. Elissa ran after him.

"No, oh please no," she said. "Don't say anything to her. Don't do anything. Please. Please no."

She was snatching at his sleeve but he pushed her away and kept on, a furious determined walk. She turned and went back to the rock where he had left the rifle. She picked it up and held it in position, the butt against her shoulder, her eye at the sight. She turned the barrel toward the house, toward Florence, but Florence had gone home. Without thinking, she sighted the kitchen window and waited and waited, and then pressed the trigger. Nothing happened. She had forgotten to release the safety catch.

Voices came to her now, she could hear them shouting. The word "crazy" drifted toward her on the windless air and then "bastard". She shook her head; she would not listen.

And then—she did not know why—she turned the rifle so that the barrel pointed to her chest. She reached for the trigger, but her arms were not long enough. She crouched. She placed the gunstock on the ground. Nothing worked.

Yes, she thought, you'd have to use your toe. You put the stock on the ground, the barrel at your chest, and you push the trigger back, away from you, with a toe. It would work perfectly.

She smiled at the thought and then looked around, suddenly self-conscious. She put the rifle back, leaning it against the rock just as it had been, and she walked slowly to the house.

5

"Look, kid, you can go if you want to, but if your father finds out, don't come crying to me."

Beryl had said this to her late at night on that same Saturday

Elissa had brought her the death flowers, and now it was Saturday again, and she had been going to the Blue Spider for almost a year.

Elissa stood in front of the bathroom mirror touching her hair. She wore it in immense curls that tumbled about her head, some of them only half combed out, still springy from the rollers. Florence wore her hair this way; it was the fashion, she said. Florence helped her with everything. She had taught Elissa how to spread the thick layer of pancake makeup evenly over her face and how to blend in the little dot of rouge so that her cheekbones stood out flushed against all that pink. She had helped her pick the peasant blouse, elasticized at the shoulders, and the plaid skirt, yards and yards of material that swirled around her when she danced and that concealed her thin legs and hips. And she had taught her how to act at the Blue Spider. She called Elissa Cookie, and Elissa called her Candy. The soldiers liked their names.

She smiled at her reflection in the mirror, tipping her head from one side to the other to catch a glimpse of herself in profile. She pursed her lips the way Florence did. Minutes went by and Elissa continued to pose before the mirror, distracted from her own image by the thought of Len.

She had met him on her first Saturday at the Blue Spider. They danced once or twice that night, but she did not remember him a week later; she had been too excited, too confused. Everyone seemed to like her. They laughed and drank and danced. How could she have remembered one soldier out of so many? But when he reminded her that they had danced together only a week earlier, she was embarrassed and grateful. She fell in love with him at once. And now, every Saturday night, they drifted together early in the evening, kissing and touching in the booths and on the way home.

"He loves me," she said aloud to the mirror. She touched her hair one last time and then put on the soft pink lipstick her mother liked; she would put on the deep red just before she reached Finial Street.

"Don't get in trouble, you," her mother said.

"Oh, Ma."

"And you better get home before he does. If he finds out, he'll kill you."

"I'm always home before he is. Don't worry."

Elissa let the screen door slam behind her, but Pal had wriggled out before it closed and was wagging his stubby tail excitedly.

"No, Pal. Go back," she said. "Go back!" She stamped her foot and pointed toward the door. The dog only lowered his head and put back his ears. "Goddamn," she said. Pal began to whimper. "Ma," she shouted, "call the dog, will you? He's gonna follow me." The dog slunk into the house.

Beryl watched her daughter walk down the dirt road, her hips swaying, her curls tossing with the movements of her head. "You look nice, Elissa," she said to herself, and then turned away, back to her empty house. Pal was in her way, sniffing at the screen door. "Get out of here, damn you," she said. "Damn dog." She kicked him lightly and he yelped and ran. Suddenly she found she was angry. "Damn you!" she shouted at the dog, and then she turned and leaned against the door, watching her daughter disappear down the road to Finial Street.

At Finial Street they were waiting for her in the jeep, but Len was not with them. The two soldiers in back made room for her, and even before she sat down the jeep roared away. One soldier had his arm around her shoulders, the other put his hand on her knee; she settled in comfortably between them.

"Isn't Len coming tonight?" She tried to sound casual.

"Hey, is Len coming tonight?" The soldier repeated her question, laughter in his voice. He tightened his grip on her shoulder.

"I don't know. Is Len coming tonight?" The other picked up the question, nudging her leg with his.

"What's the joke?" she said. "What the hell's so funny?" She leaned forward. "Hey, Candy, what the hell's so funny?"

"Wouldn't you like to know?" Florence said, rolling her eyes.

"Come on, tell me."

Florence leaned back and whispered in her ear. "Len's gonna get a car. And you know what *that* means." She laughed wildly, rocking from side to side, wriggling against the driver. "Woo woo."

"Woo woo," Elissa said, laughing, but her heart lurched, and she could feel the blood rushing in her arms and legs.

She loved Len. She loved the feel of him as he pressed up against her in the booths or when they kissed in the jeep on the way home. She would twist around in the seat so that her whole body would be touching his, and then she would move gently back and forth so she could feel him thrusting against her. She wanted to be naked under him.

She looked down at her lap and then at the lap of the soldier next to her. She could see that soft bulge. She could reach over and put her hand right on it. What would he do? She didn't even know his name, and yet she could reach out and do something like that. She would, too, someday. She would tonight, maybe, with Len.

"See anything you like?" the soldier said, shifting a little on the seat. "If you were a squirrel I'd be worried."

"Bastard," she said, and hit him in the ribs with her elbow. She tossed back her head and began to sing the "Pocaluma Polka." It was going to be a perfect night. Nothing could spoil it. She was still singing when they reached the Blue Spider and went in.

Elissa was thrilled by the air of excitement in the place. Everyone was in motion, talking and laughing. There were some girls in the booths already, but most of them were dancing, and there were soldiers lounging against the jukebox waiting for their turn. Someone called to her from one of the back booths. She waved to him and laughed. She was dancing, gliding backward to the heavy beat of the music, humming. She could feel the soldier's hands moving on her shoulder and at the small of her back. She didn't care. Let him. She was dancing with someone else now, she could feel his thighs against hers. She was floating, and always there was the music blaring and bodies touching hers. She was safe here. She was alive. Someone handed her a can of beer and she was surprised at the sharp bitter taste. She took a long slug from the can and everyone applauded.

"Jesus, are you ever the one!" Florence said to her, and then she whispered something to one of the soldiers. They laughed together and then he whispered to her. "You pig," she said, and pushed against his chest with her fist, laughing. They sat down in a booth.

Len had come in and was standing by the jukebox waiting for the music to stop. They were dancing to the "Chicken Bop," and every few steps the girl would pull away from the boy and do a little hop. It was a popular dance because it gave the girls a chance to show what they were made of, Len had once told her. Elissa moved away from her partner, hopped, and returned. He grinned and said, "What've you got down there?" He pulled at the elastic on her blouse.

"Pig," she said. She was flirting more than she would have if she had seen Len come in.

She swung out from her partner once again, did her little hop, and returned, and this time he said, "You've really got something. Let's take a look." And he pulled again at the elastic. The blouse slipped from her left shoulder, and she pushed it back easily with a flick of her thumb. But she was annoyed.

"Come on," she said. "Cut it."

The dance was about to end. "I'll be good," he said. He held her tight against him, but when she swung out and returned for the last time, like a small boy he said, "Just one little peek," and he pulled at the elastic.

She stopped dancing and stood there. "Now look what you done," she said. The elastic had broken and her blouse drooped low on the left shoulder.

"Let's see, let's see," he said, being funny. The music had stopped and everyone was beginning to stare.

"Come on, let's get out of here," Len said. He came between her and her partner.

"Hey, hold on there, soldier," he said. "You stealing my little girl friend here?" And he pushed Len to the side.

"Look at this. Look what he done," Elissa was saying. "How can I go home with my blouse like this?"

"Quit shoving," Len said to the soldier, and took Elissa by the arm.

The soldier spun him around. "You didn't answer my question, friend. You stealing my little girl friend here?" He waited for an answer. "Huh?" He pushed Len in the chest with the flat of his hand. "Huh?" Another push. "What do you say, soldier boy?"

The crowd around them had fallen silent, the faces hungry for a fight. Len glanced at them, and knew what was expected of him. But he didn't want a fight. Not now.

"Don't try that again," he said, and spat on the floor.

"Try what? Try this?" He pushed Len harder. "Why, this is the easiest thing in the world, no trying involved." He pushed him harder still.

And then before anyone knew what happened, before anyone could holler "fight," Len lashed out with his right fist and caught the soldier on the side of the head. He lurched back, but as he fell, he struck the other side of his head on one of the upright beams. It made only a dull thudding sound. He slid down the beam to a sitting position, a look of surprise on his face, blood beginning to drip from the side of his head. Len took Elissa's arm and pushed her to the door.

"Hey, no rough stuff," the bartender was shouting. Everyone was talking loudly. "Who got hit?" "Who did it?"

They stood for a moment outside the door, Elissa holding the blouse together with her hand. They were breathless, flushed with excitement.

"I got a car," Len said.

"I know it."

He paused, and she stood there fiddling with the material of her blouse.

"Do you want to?"

"Yes. Do you?"

Laughing, they ran to the car.

"Yellow bastard," they heard the soldier shout as they drove off. "Come on back and fight, you bastard."

They drove out of town, out beyond the houses and the fields and the base, deep into the pocked and sweltering desert. They were silent the whole way, an odd formality between them. Finally Len stopped the car and they got out.

"This looks all right," he said. "What do you think?"

"Yes, this is fine," she said. What had happened? He was a

stranger, she thought, he was just someone else she did not know. But I love him and he loves me. We're going to make love, she told herself, trying to recapture the excitement of the Blue Spider. He was naked now, standing on the blanket he had spread over the sand. He was caressing his fat stomach.

"Come on," he said. "Get those clothes off, for Christ sake. We haven't got all night."

They made love and afterward she said, "Is that all?" It had happened so quickly, just a brief hard pain that spread upward into her chest, taking her breath away, and then nothing more.

"What do you mean, is that all?"

"I mean, should we go home now?"

"Oh, yeah," he said. And as he picked up the blanket and walked to the car, he added, "Hey, uh, thanks a lot."

"That's all right," she said.

They were silent as he drove her home.

* * *

Luke had been home for more than an hour. He had gone upstairs and sat, waiting, on Elissa's bed and then he had come down.

"Where is she?" he asked Beryl.

"She's out for a walk. She was too hot up there."

"Yeah, I hear she's hot up there. I hear she's hot down at the Blue Spider too."

"Who says?" He was drunk, she knew, but canny drunk. It was best not to antagonize him. "Men gossip," she said. "They just make things up."

"My own daughter, a friggin whore. I have to hear about it at the Oaks. My wife don't tell me. Oh no, she's helping her do it."

"Who said . . ."

"It's been going on for a year, they tell me. 'Hey, Gerriter,' he says to me, 'I hear your daughter's getting it plenty.' I call him a dirty liar and he says, 'No, it's true.' So I'm gonna punch him in the face and they tell me, 'No, Gerriter, it's true. She's down there every Saturday.' And there I was listening to them laugh about my own daughter. I'll teach her. I'll beat her to an inch of her life."

"I let her go. I'm the one. I said she could go as long as she got home before you did. So if you're gonna blame anybody, it's me."

"Yeah, I should beat you too. I should have years ago."

"You're not going to beat anybody, Luke Gerriter. Get that straight."

"I'm not gonna be made a fool of by my own daughter. I'm gonna teach her a lesson." He stormed into the kitchen and took a beer from the refrigerator. Beryl followed him. " 'She's getting it plenty,' he says to me."

"Don't you touch that girl."

"I'll touch anybody I goddamn please."

They stared at each other in silence for a moment, and then Luke took a long slug from the beer can.

Beryl spoke very slowly. "If you put a hand on her, I warn you, I'll kill you." She continued to stare at him for a moment, and then she went to the bedroom.

She sat by the window trembling. They had not fought for almost a year now, not since the day he had sent Elissa to her with the flowers. She had changed since then, she knew it. Something strange had happened inside her and she found herself, despite the stored anger between them, wanting him, wanting him with her in bed. She could not tell him this, but there were times when she ached, when she lay in bed listening to him snore and had to keep herself from going to his cot and saying, "Come to bed with me, I want you." And now it was all going to change again, within an hour, as soon as Elissa got home. She could foresee it, the accusations, the heavy hands, the screaming. She shook her head to clear it.

In the kitchen Luke had finished his beer and took down from the pantry shelf the bottle of whisky he kept there. He sat at the kitchen table and watched the whisky rise in the tumbler; he filled it only half full. He put his head on the table to rest, to wait for her. As the time passed and the whisky sank in the bottle, he wept for himself as a betrayed father, for his daughter being used by filthy soldiers, for everything. He would grow angry and violent, pace around the kitchen, cursing and threatening to beat her half to death. And after a while he would sit down again. He dozed fitfully. By the time the small gray car turned off Finial Street onto the dirt road, Luke had finished most of the bottle and was thoroughly, violently, drunk.

* * *

The car stopped in front of the house and the two people inside sat there in silence. They had not spoken once since leaving the desert. Finally Len cleared his throat.

"Um, there's something I should tell you. I'm being shipped out soon."

"Oh." As if she had expected it.

"Yeah, this week. They're sending me overseas."

"Oh."

"Yeah. Maybe I should have told you before. Maybe you wouldn't have wanted to do it."

"No, that's all right," she said.

"Well, anyway, it was, um, great."

"Yes," she said.

She got out of the car and closed the door softly.

"See you around," he said and drove off, fast.

"That's all right," she said, and drifted toward the door, her hand at the shoulder of her torn blouse. Vaguely she noticed that the light was on behind the screen door. She couldn't breathe very well. She stopped by the evergreen tree, bending into its spiky branches to inhale the bitter smell. The screen door creaked, but she did not turn around.

Her head jerked sharply back and there was a tearing pain in her shoulder as Luke grabbed her arm from behind and pulled her into the light.

"Look at you, you whore, you pig," he said softly, staring at the curls and the makeup and the crimson slash at her mouth. He slapped her hard on the face. In the silence, the crack of his hand against her skin was like a gunshot, and involuntarily he drew away from her, hesitating for a moment. And then he saw the blouse. "Look, look!" he said. "Is that what happens in the cars, huh, they can't wait to get at you so they have to rip your clothes off."

Elissa backed away from him. He was crazy drunk. He might do anything.

"Or do you like it that way? Damned whore," he said, "some like it that way. Do you? Huh? Do you like it?" And with one hand he reached out and tore her blouse down the front. His anger grew as he looked at her. "Look at you," he screamed. "Look at you." He tore at her brassiere, and as she struggled it came loose in his hand. She stood stripped to the waist in the light shining through the screen door. "Whore," he said, "pig," and slapped at her breasts, pulling her closer and closer to him as they struggled. She was screaming, pushing him away, and he was calling her whore, whore, while his neck and chest heaved with the violence of what he was doing. He felt fists on his back and he heard someone calling his name and then something struck his head.

"Luke, Luke," Beryl was saying. "Luke."

He took his hands from Elissa and turned, with the face of a stranger, to Beryl. He looked at her, confused.

"Get in the house," she said, her voice firm and low.

"She . . ." Luke said, pointing to his daughter.

"I know. Get in the house."

Luke went up the stairs slowly, bent like an old man, never having noticed the pistol in her hand.

Elissa and Beryl looked at one another, uncertain, questioning.

"Nothing happened, did it," Beryl said. Elissa continued to look at her. "Nothing happened," she insisted.

"No. Nothing happened."

"I know," Beryl said, "I know," and she threw her arms around the girl, sobbing uncontrollably. "Nothing happened. Nothing. Nothing happened."

6

It was almost October and still the heat was unbearable. Luke wiped the sweat from his forehead with the back of his hand and then mopped his plate with a piece of bread, swooping down on it to catch the drippings.

"How come she's sick again?" he asked. "What's the matter with her?"

Beryl pushed back her plate. "You want another beer?" She rose to get it.

"What's the matter with the kid?"

She placed the beer can at his side and sat down at the table facing him. "She's pregnant."

"Oh no," he said, and groaned.

"She told me this afternoon. She's over three months."

Luke sat staring at his empty plate, his hands at his head. After a minute Beryl saw his shoulders shake. He was crying.

"How do you think I felt?" she said. "I told her she's gonna be punished and good. I feel like she tore something right out of me, like she killed something I had, the only thing I had."

His shoulders shook again. He said nothing.

The clock ticked above the table. They could hear Pal upstairs, as his nails clicked against the wooden floor. Beryl glanced at the ceiling and waited for Luke to say something. Finally she couldn't stand the silence any longer.

"It's not yours," she said.

He looked up at her, shocked.

"It's not your baby. I asked her."

He shook his head and looked back down at his plate. In the three months that had passed since he beat Elissa, none of them ever mentioned what had happened.

"Well, I had to know, didn't I? After that . . ."

"Yes," he said. She could barely hear it.

"Do you want to know something? Do you?" There was fright in her voice, and he looked up at her finally.

"What?"

"Do you know what I felt first of all? I was jealous."

He stared at her.

"You don't know what it's been like," she said. "Oh Jesus, sometimes I want to just die."

"It's not mine," he said. "I was drunk that time. I didn't know what I was doing."

"I know," she said. "Nothing happened anyway. Nothing happened."

There was a long silence between them and, tentatively, she moved her arm forward on the table until her fingers touched his. He did not move away.

"Can I tell you something?" she said.

He moved one of his fingers against hers.

"Sometimes I want it now. With you."

After a long moment he took her hand in his. "Oh Christ," he said, "what a mess." And for the first time in years, they went to the bedroom to make love.

* * *

Upstairs Elissa lay in her bed, one arm across her stomach. She studied the boards in the slanted roof above her head, and whenever Pal put his muzzle against her, she scratched behind his ears. But she noticed nothing, was aware of nothing.

At first, after that night with Len, she had tried to understand what had happened. He didn't love her, she knew that, but that hadn't mattered. Not that he was going away either. It was something different. Everything seemed to have come to an end—the excitement of going to the Spider, men brushing against her, touching her, knowing that something was going to happen, that it was all going to be different. But nothing was going to be different now. By the time she discovered she was pregnant, not even that mattered very much. That seemed only to prove what she already knew. She was trapped forever in the sweltering heat, fighting for a breath of air.

* * *

Around midnight they awoke and made love once again. Luke collapsed against her, breathing hard, and then rolled away, half asleep already.

"She's got to be punished," Beryl said. "She's got to be taught a lesson."

"I'll shoot her dog," Luke said. "She loves the dog."

"No. No, that's not enough."

There was a moment of silence.

"I'll make her shoot it," he said.

"Tomorrow."

Before dawn Luke walked to town and borrowed the Garners' car. He was back before the sun was fully up. Beryl had prepared a large breakfast for them and they ate it, as they always did, in silence.

Afterward Beryl said, "I told your father."

"You got to be punished," he said. "You know that."

Elissa pushed her hair back from her face but said nothing.

"We're gonna shoot that dog of yours. You're gonna shoot it, that is."

Elissa nodded.

"Now you're gonna take us out to where he did it and you're gonna show us the exact spot, and then you're gonna shoot that dog."

"You killed something I had," Beryl said, "and now you're gonna do the same."

Elissa nodded. It was all crazy. Nothing mattered.

The sun was high when they passed the last of the farms and took the road to the airbase.

"Left here," Elissa said, numb. She stroked the dog and looked out the window. Miles and miles of sand, with the sun beating down. Nothing could live here.

"Where is it?" Luke said. "It must be around here somewhere."

How could you tell, she thought, everything was the same. In a few minutes she said, "Here. Here's the place."

They got out of the car and stood by it awkwardly, looking around them. No one would ever hear a gunshot out here. They walked a long distance from the car until Luke said, "Where are you going? I thought you said it was here."

"Yes, it is here. It's right here."

Luke drove a stake deep into the sand and tied the dog's leash to it. He walked five paces distant, readying the gun. He cocked it, examined the shells, snapped it shut. Only twenty-twos, but at such close range enough to kill a dog. He released the safety catch and handed Elissa the pistol.

"Do it," he said. "Do it or we just drive off and leave you. It's your punishment."

Luke and Beryl moved off and stood at a distance, watching.

Elissa looked at the pistol, turned it over in her hand, and then looked at Pal, who wagged his tail and tried to come to her. She looked up at the sky into the blinding sun and thought she saw a cloud coming, perhaps it meant rain, but it was just the sun against her eyes, and when she looked back at Pal she saw only a blazing dog shape against the sand. Slowly, evenly, she raised the small gun, placing the barrel firmly beneath her right ear.

The only sound in the desert was the dog whimpering in the terrible heat.

Part Two

FOX AND SWAN

It SEEMED the cold would never let up. For over a week the temperature had been below freezing, and for most of that time it had hovered around zero. Francis hated cold weather, his long, stringy body responding to it with unmanly shivers. Nor could he afford the winter coat he needed.

Christ, will it ever end, he asked himself, and he pulled his scarf tighter. It was a long, striped scarf worn like a college student's—outside the jacket, hanging down in front and in back—even though he knew he was too old for that sort of thing.

A girl turned to stare. A winter hippy, a rarity, she wore an enormous black cloak with silk frogging and fur buttons. Over this her blond hair hung in ropes almost to her waist. She squinted at him through tinted granny glasses.

"Groovy beard," she said, raising her hands to her face. "You look like a fox, man." And then she added, "Sexy!"

He smiled at her; in Harvard Square you could expect anything. He felt at home here, anonymous.

Francis Xavier Madden, Stud, he said to himself and shook his head a little at the mockery.

It was not altogether mockery, however, even though he himself was oblivious to his looks. His beard had made the difference. Because he had no money to throw away on haircuts, he wore his hair long, the thick straight copper turning a ruddy brown at his mouth and chin, with a strand of gold here and there. His beard emphasized his heavy lips and his curiously protruding teeth in such a way that girls—at least the ones he met in Harvard

Square—found him unusually attractive. They often stared at him, many even spoke. Still, he was always astonished whenever any- one referred to him as sexy. Sex had never been one of his major concerns.

A sexy fox, he thought. A nice image. He had spent the entire afternoon turning over in his mind ideas for a story about a fox and swans. He had not thought of introducing sex. A sexy fox.

He recited the clipping once again. "At Southampton, fish were caught and frozen in the ice, their heads jutting out. Starving seabirds swooped down to peck at them. And swans froze in a river at Christchurch, Hampshire, their legs trapped in ice. Foxes glided across to devour them."

He had found it in the morning *Globe* and, for some reason he could not specify, he was deeply moved by it. In the human reaction to such inhuman cold there must be a story, he told him- self. By the end of the afternoon he had the beginnings of a plot. A woman, a perfect Catholic, would be on her way to perform a "charity" and thereby wreck a reputation. She would pause at a little footbridge over the river—Christchurch River, since the story was to be heavily ironic—and would watch while a fox crept from among the trees and devoured the trapped swan. She would then continue on her way as purposeful and righteous as before. Or perhaps she would be changed by what she saw? No, people never were. He wondered if the "Christchurch" part might be too much. Well, he could work that out later.

He passed the Coop and deliberately looked the other way. No sense checking out overcoats he couldn't afford. That would only set in motion his endless mental book-balancing: possible income measured against definite expenses. He had not realized about money. Well, first sex, then money. You've got to have priorities.

If only he could sell the story. Christ, if only he could *write* it. He told himself to stop worrying, it wasn't healthy. Besides, this story was going to write itself. He had begun it with ease, and would have liked to continue writing, but Caryl was expecting him and she needed . . . well, at least he could read her the first page, which she would like, and tomorrow he could begin work with, with what? With . . . He paused, waiting for a car to turn out of Church Street.

"Cold, sweet Christ, it's cold," he said aloud.

"It's too cold even to snow." The girl in the cloak had followed, and stopped with him now at the street corner. She was hopping from foot to foot to keep warm. "At first I thought you were a young guy."

"So did I. At first."

"But you aren't. Funny, you got a groovy beard."

He smiled, and immediately wished he hadn't. He knew she would ask for a quarter.

"Got a quarter?" She squinted at him with little pig eyes. They were pink. Or perhaps it was the glasses that made them look pink.

What's the use, he thought. A gust of wind swept around the corner as he tugged at his glove. He could feel the ice seeping up his arm and spreading across his chest. He wanted to cry.

"Here," he said, dropping the quarter into her red mitten. He could never refuse anything he was asked for.

"You're a groove," she said. "See ya." She did a strange little pirouette that made her cloak billow out and then swirl, snug, around her body. She returned to her position at the Coop.

It would be something to tell Caryl. She would enjoy it, but then she enjoyed everything about him, most of all sleeping with him. What a crazy situation, he thought.

* * *

The crazy situation had begun normally enough a year earlier when they were graduate students at Harvard.

Caryl Henderson was a tall plain girl who at twenty-eight decided that her chances of marriage were slender, and if she wanted to have any kind of fulfilling life, she had better set about making it herself. And so, once she was accepted at Harvard, she quit her teaching job at Cambridge High and entered the Ph.D. program in English. She had resolved upon intellectual happiness, the doors to other kinds being closed to her.

Francis Madden had long since chosen his vocation when he came to Harvard. He was a Jesuit. After three years studying theology, in the year he was to be ordained, he began to ask himself—

as he often had before, but this time with peculiar insistence—
if this were what he really wanted to do with his life. Too many
of his Jesuit friends had been ordained to the priesthood only to
leave and get married within a year or two. Not that route for
him. And so he postponed his ordination and, after a great deal
of ecclesiastical maneuvering, arranged to work for his Ph.D. at
Harvard while making up his mind about the priesthood.

Caryl and Francis became friends by the accident of sharing
classes. She was in her fourth year of studies but, as teaching assistant to Professor Barker, she regularly attended his lectures.
Neither Caryl nor Francis was in love with the other, nor with
anyone else for that matter, nor did they think of falling in love.
They were just friends, older than their fellow students, and they
shared common interests. The difference was that Francis hated
graduate studies and Caryl loved them.

At the end of his first year, then, Francis decided to quit school
altogether and, almost as an afterthought, to quit the Jesuits
as well. The academic game had brought home to him a truth he
had only half suspected: all his life he had done what other people
thought he should do, whether or not it was the right thing for
him. He had begun work on a Ph.D. not because he wanted it but
because in the Jesuit order a Ph.D. was the only criterion for intellectual acceptability. For similar reasons—because it was in itself
a good and difficult thing to do and because Catholic families
could aspire to no more blessed state than having a son who was
a priest—he had very nearly been ordained. Now, realizing what
his motives had been, he turned his back on both and walked out
free, he was sure, into a whole new life.

Caryl was delighted that he had found his freedom, she said,
delighted that he could now spend all his time writing. She was in
fact more delighted than she could reasonably explain to herself.
She was a devout Catholic and a plain woman and he was prac-
tically a priest; it had never occurred to her until now that during
their frequent lunches and their walks through Cambridge Common she might be falling in love. She had cut her hair, it is true,
and wore it in a soft halo about her face, where before she had
pulled it back into a tight little bun. And that because he had once
admired that girl on television, Mary Tyler Moore, or somebody.

And she had begun to wear lipstick, too, which he liked. But that wasn't the same as falling in love, she told herself.

Just before he left the Jesuits Francis sold his first short story to *The New Yorker*. Having never before published anything, he was more elated by the acceptance than by the money, and so it meant little to him that Superiors let him keep the five hundred dollars and bettered their gesture by giving him two hundred more. When he phoned Caryl with his good news, she cried with pleasure. She had good news as well—she had just passed her comprehensive exams—but tactfully she postponed telling him until later. She invited him to dinner to celebrate.

"A coming out party," he said.

"A recognition party," she said.

The dinner was an unqualified success. Caryl was not a good cook and, having the wisdom to recognize her own shortcomings, had concentrated her efforts on preparing a few simple dishes well: she served him steak and baked potatoes and a colorful display of fresh vegetables. Francis had thought to bring wine, a good Pinot Noir he would not be able to afford in the future. And she always had scotch on hand. Furthermore, Woolf remained in the bathroom during dinner. Woolf—at first called Virginia, until his true sex had made itself known—was a dingy alley cat Caryl had adopted for the purpose, she said, of destroying her furniture. Woolf resented newcomers and generally sulked in the bathroom when company came.

They laughed a great deal and toasted Francis' story and *The New Yorker* and the story again. They drank more than they were accustomed to, feeling adventurous and successful, what with her Ph.D. exams completed and his writing career begun.

After dinner Francis read his story aloud, as later he was to read everything aloud to Caryl. It was less a story than a slightly fictionalized reminiscence of his days in the novitiate, but it had a certain amount of action and made some telling points about how the religious life shapes a man's character. Caryl was enchanted.

They toasted the story again and, when they were about to toast *The New Yorker*, Francis kissed her instead. It was a light kiss on the mouth, but he lingered there a moment and was astonished to feel Caryl's lips part and her arms slip away from him and tighten around his neck. He felt it was time to loosen his hold on her, but she seemed content where she was and so, rather than appear rude, he began to explore her teeth with his tongue. He began to feel feverish.

"No one kisses like you," she said, gasping, as she pulled her mouth away and clung even tighter to him. He smiled to himself. Never having done this before, he was glad he had done it right. Then he reflected that perhaps she had never done it before either, so how would she know? Somehow, he found that encouraging. He turned off the lamp.

"I don't know what I'm supposed to do," she said. "Just tell me what to do."

They slumped in each other's arms. Pushing the pillows about and nudging hips and knees, they managed finally to get into a semireclining position. They kissed again and then once more. Francis began to discover that a certain finesse was required, force and enthusiasm being insufficient to sustain the sweetness of the pleasure.

"It's like a symphony," she said, and he laughed loudly until the couch, which at night doubled as her bed, shook with his laughter. He was pleased with his newly discovered expertise. "Stop it," she said. "You're laughing at me."

"No, I'm laughing at me." He kissed her lightly on the neck. "Biology is fun."

He removed his tie and his shirt, he explained, because it was too warm. He drained his glass while he was up.

"I'm a little drunk," he confided.

She said nothing, only slipped her hand beneath his tee shirt, and felt his body grow tense. "What?" He didn't answer. "Shouldn't I do that?" She began to remove her hand just as he slipped his own under her sweater and began to caress her breasts. She unhooked her brassiere for him.

What in God's name am I doing? he thought, but even as he thought it, he got out of bed and began to remove his trousers.

"What are you doing?"

"Don't worry, I won't hurt you. I promise. I'm just going to hang these on the chair. They're my best suit and I don't want to get them wrinkled."

Francis folded the trousers neatly and was about to place them over a chair back when Woolf, who had been curled comfortably in the seat, arched his back enormously and hissed. The cat sprang from the chair and disappeared into the little kitchen.

"Damn cat scared the hell out of me."

He turned and found that she had removed her skirt and sweater. She was sitting on the edge of the bed, looking at him, trusting him absolutely. Though she had always been unusually modest, she felt no embarrassment whatsoever with him.

"Woolf is jealous," she said.

Francis felt suddenly awkward. He took her hands in his own and she began to rise just as he began to ease himself on to the couch. They collided and, in her attempt to sit down again and in his to stand, they plopped to the couch in a tangle of arms and legs, Francis rapping his head soundly against the window frame.

"Ouch," he said, his confusion localized for the moment. "I banged my head."

"It's the window frame."

"I know it's the window frame."

She rubbed the back of his head, which he lowered to her breasts, incredibly white and smooth, just as he had imagined breasts would be, though until then he had never imagined Caryl's. It's like a novel, he thought, and kissed her breasts the way they did in novels. He moved closer to her, his knee between her legs, his right arm a clumsy lump under her shoulders. There seemed to be an awful lot of arms and legs around.

From his study of moral and pastoral theology, Francis knew a great deal about sexual play. Books, however, differ considerably from experience and, as he slipped off her panties, he was totally confused as to what went where. Caryl had not had the benefit of theological training and so she lay there, passive and grateful.

"Move this leg here," he whispered.

But as Caryl moved her leg and Francis edged closer to her, Woolf with a terrible hissing sound sprang from the desk onto the bed.

"Christ!" Francis was terrified. Recovering, he reared back to push the cat from the bed, but as he did, his arm caught the window curtains and pulled. They came tumbling down on the bed, the curtain rods with them. Woolf screamed and tried to bolt, but he was trapped in the curtains and his struggles only entangled them all further.

What an idiot I am, he thought, wrestling his feet to the floor, where at once he tripped on the cat and landed on his hands and knees. Caryl's delighted laughter made him feel even more foolish. He vowed this would never happen again.

Caryl spent the next day waiting for him to return. The experience had been the most beautiful of her life, except for the funny part, but even that was good. Everything with Francis was good. That morning, as she did every morning, she received Communion, having first considered that her catechism said last night was sinful and having reconsidered that her catechism was wrong. Love is good and beautiful, she told herself, and she could not in conscience confess what they had done as sinful. Sin had no part in this whatsoever. She waited for him, then, to return in the evening.

Francis had stumbled home confused, and a little pleased with what he took for his sexual prowess. The next morning, however, he went to confession, resolving to see Caryl that same evening to explain that if this ever happened again, they would no longer be able to see one another. That day was a Jesuit feast, however, and when Francis arrived at Caryl's apartment he had already had three scotches, two wines, and a brandy. His opinion of himself had improved measurably, and he was feeling very consciously male. He kissed her as she opened the door.

It was exactly one hour and seventeen minutes later that, in bed once more, he eased his body away from hers. They had found the act of love easy and natural, once Francis had put his textbook knowledge aside, and they had rejoiced in it. They lay there, smiling at one another. It was only much later that night that the possibility of Caryl's being pregnant occurred to them.

For the next two weeks they lived in a state of continual panic. Papers came from Rome dispensing Francis from his vows and freeing him from all obligations to the Society of Jesus, but Francis scarcely noticed them. He moved from Jesuit life to the life of a layman almost unaware of what was happening to him. His entire consciousness, like Caryl's, was focused on one event: her next period.

He would marry her, he thought, and legitimize the baby. She would have to drop her dissertation, or at least hide out in the late days of her pregnancy. He would have to get a job. That took care of his writing career, Goddamn it.

She wanted more than anything to marry him, but not in this way, not with the knowledge that if he had to give up his writing, he would always resent her. She wanted him to be free to write, and free, if he chose, to marry her. But what about the baby?

The two weeks passed, a psychiatric study in guilt and responsibility for the two of them, and then—just when they had all but named the baby and provided for its education—they found she was not pregnant. Terrified at their new freedom, they celebrated her period with dinner at Barney's. Afterward, they returned to her apartment, where she wanted to make love again, but Francis would not.

"Can't we just go to bed and lie there together?"

He frowned and said nothing.

"We won't do anything bad. It isn't as if we would do something bad."

He was about to ask her if she realized he had a vow of chastity when he himself realized he had one no longer. So instead he told her, "We can't. You know what will happen."

"We won't have . . . you know . . . intercourse. I hate that word. It's the most beautiful thing in the world and they call it that awful word. But we won't do that."

"It isn't intercourse that makes it a sin. It's the whole thing. It's what you're saying about your feeling for the other person when you go to bed together. It means you give yourself to that person and to no other. No other at all."

He was trying to remember his theology, the carefully elaborated reasons that demonstrate even to the unbeliever exactly why premarital sex is sinful. Hearing himself now, he was not convinced.

"Well, you aren't giving yourself to anyone but me." She did not see the problem.

"But I can't. I can't stand the guilt the next morning. And in confession they'll just tell me I have to break off. That's what they always do."

"I don't feel guilty at all. I feel wonderful. And I don't tell it in confession. I would if I thought it was wrong. But I don't. Not if we don't have intercourse."

And so that night they went to bed together and did not have intercourse. Francis, who had roamed her body and enjoyed emissions three times, dutifully went off to confession the next morning. Caryl, however, was blessed with an astonishing dispensation of conscience, or so it seemed to Francis, and she rose bright and holy, ready for Mass and Communion.

Their relations continued in much this way throughout the summer. As Francis' love for her had changed Caryl into an attractive woman, his physical affection for her made her a free one. Her years and years of strict Catholic upbringing fell away in that one night. She was liberated. Surprisingly, her sense of freedom extended beyond herself and, where she had wished for nothing better than to marry Francis, she now wished his happiness above all else. It was this selflessness, though he would never have guessed it, that made him most uneasy.

Francis, on the other hand, felt daily more constricted, more obliged. The Catholic training, the involuted mental discipline of the Jesuits, which he had happily and with ease cast off in his first love for Caryl, returned to him now and possessed him completely. He was haunted by a sense of sin he had not known in years. He felt he should break off with Caryl, but she was all he had, and he might yet come to love her almost as much as she loved him. Still, he felt obliged to visit her often and to phone each day, and this worried him. It seemed to deny his freedom. And when he was with her they would invariably begin kissing and petting and then that would mean another guilty morning and a trip to the confessional. By this time he was rotating priests, but they all told him the same thing: unless he planned marriage, he should end the relationship. Furthermore, she seemed oblivious to his maddening need for something more than just being naked in bed with her. This, he thought, is what they really mean by the frustration of a faculty. He had left the Jesuits for freedom to be himself, and he was being something he could not even recognize. He had quit graduate studies to write, and he spent most of his time worrying about not writing. Summer passed this way, and now much of the winter.

* * *

It was, he thought, a crazy situation. He pulled his scarf tighter as he left the Cambridge Common and approached her apartment. It seemed the cold would never let up.

"Sweet, hello," she said, stepping into his arms. It amazed him how beautiful she had become.

He held her tightly, half aware of her breasts warm against him, half aware of the door still open at his back. I can never enjoy anything, he thought.

"Hello, hello," she whispered.

"Hi." He gave her the expected response and closed the door. "Wow, it's cold."

"Sit. I'll make you a drink." She caressed his beard for a moment before she disappeared into the little kitchen.

"Hey, you know, there was this girl who asked me for a quarter, followed me actually. She had funny little pig eyes and a wild cape . . ."

"That's Magdalena," she said from the kitchen. "Don't you know her? She makes a fortune in the Square."

"Magdalena?"

"Her name's not really Magdalena. It's Margaret Ann or something, but she fancies Magdalena, so everybody calls her that."

"How do you know her? How do you know all that?" He was vaguely offended. He had hoped to please her with his description.

"Oh, I know a few things."

Handing him the drink, she posed for a minute with one hand on her hip and her breasts thrust forward, a new thing with her.

"Well, tell me about your writing," she said, suspecting she had annoyed him. "Did you write today?" She gave him her total attention; for her nobody, nothing else, existed at that moment.

He sipped his drink. "Good scotch," he said. He could not afford good scotch himself, his seven hundred dollars having been consumed by rent for his shabby two rooms on Green Street and by restaurants he could not afford and gifts he should not have given.

"You did write, I can tell. You're like a Cheshire. You're like poor old Woolfykins when he had caught a mouse." She had had Woolf put away once it became clear that he and Francis were incompatible. "Tell me. Read it to me."

"It's kinda good, I think. I think I'm really onto something."

He recited the news clipping about the cold on Christchurch River, the fish and the seabirds, the swan and the fox. He told her that there would be a woman, a very particular kind of woman, who would witness the murder and then go away unchanged. Or maybe it should be a priest; he wasn't sure. And the tone would be heavily ironic, light on the surface but deep irony.

"Read it," she said. He wrote better than he explained, and she wanted very much to like the story.

"You don't like the plot?"

"Read it."

"You don't like something. I can tell."

As it happened, she did have reservations about the story. He had never been to England, and there were no swans at Harvard. Besides, why so artificial a contrivance? But she refused to let herself think about these things.

"I love it. Read it."

"O.K." He cleared his throat, sipped his drink, cleared his throat again.

" 'She was a perfect Catholic. In 1968 few Catholics were perfect, but she was perfect. She went to Mass every Sunday, of course —which everybody did—but besides that, she talked to Lutherans about religion and organized card parties for the Passionist retreats and staged, at considerable expense to her nerves and to her family, fashion shows for the benefit of the Stigmatine Fathers. She was a perfect Catholic at a time when few Catholic women were.' "

He looked up, dissatisfied at the writing. It had seemed to work before, but now it seemed all wrong.

"You don't like it, do you," he said.

"Frank, I love it. I like the 'at great expense to her nerves and to her family.' That's really good."

"What is it that you don't like? Is it the Catholic business?"

"Well, you might eventually want to write about something else." She spoke apologetically. "You do keep returning to that over and over."

"I happen to *be* Catholic, is all. And I don't like screwing around unless I'm getting married."

"Read the rest of the story, Frank." She never argued with him.

"It isn't that I don't love you." He wondered if he did love her. She was lovely and intelligent and utterly selfless. And those fabulous breasts. Marrying her was not the problem; feeling he *had* to was the problem. Or did he imagine it? "It isn't that."

"What is it?" She asked the question simply. It was not a challenge.

"It's . . . I mean . . . *you* want to marry *me*." He waited. "Don't you."

"Yes, I want to marry you. But only if you want to marry me. I want you to be as free and happy as I am."

"Free! Christ, this is impossible." He stood and looked around for his jacket. "I'm going to go, Caryl. I'll come back some time. I shouldn't have come tonight. It was a bad idea, the whole thing. I'm preoccupied, I guess, with that Goddamned story."

He brushed his lips against hers and left.

The wind across the Common cut his face and neck. Francis tugged at his scarf, but that did no good. The cold would never end, he thought.

And what on earth had propelled them into such an incredible argument? Who had first mentioned marriage? He tried to reconstruct the scene. She hadn't liked the story because of something about the swans. Had she actually said that, or was she just thinking it? No, she hadn't said it. But he knew, he knew. He could change the swan to a fish and the fox to a seabird; that would be more plausible. And he could locate the story on the Charles instead of Christchurch River. What had come over her anyway? Why should he feel so obliged to her? Trapped, almost.

"Got a quarter?" Magdalena squinted up at him, not smiling, merely making her request.

"Why? Why should I give you a quarter?" Francis was amazed at the sound of his own voice, raw with hatred.

"I need bread, man."

"Why don't you go work for it instead of pestering people in the street. What makes you think the whole world owes you a living just because you've got the brass to ask for it. Who the hell do you think you are, anyhow."

"Look, man, I do my thing. You do your thing, right? I ask for a quarter, you don't want to give a quarter, so say no. Who needs a speech?"

She stood there, having somehow confounded him with her logic, while he strode angrily away, not to Green Street but to the Charles.

"Sexy beard," she said. "He's a fox."

His anger made him forget the cold, and he walked rapidly down Boylston Street to the Anderson Bridge. He did not know why. He glided out on the ice, easing himself along gingerly at first, and then walking firmly once he discovered it was safe. He had not known that rivers freeze.

Only after he had walked half the distance to the Weeks Bridge did he become conscious of what he was doing: He was searching for a fish frozen in the ice, "their heads jutting out," he recited. But that was absurd. What on earth would a fish be doing with its head out of water? Still, in the story it would be a wonderful Christ symbol. He smiled to himself. She was right, he thought.

When he reached the Weeks Bridge, he left the ice. With a feeling that he was shouldering the inevitable, he retraced his steps to Harvard Square, where he waited impatiently for Magdalena to make her appearance. He looked in the newspaper store, but she was not there, nor was she in the theater lobby. She was probably home by now, doing her thing. It was too cold to wait any longer.

He set off quickly up Boylston Street. At the corner of Church, he paused. There was an ashcan standing next to a mailbox. He took out the folded page of his story, dropped it in the ashcan, and then for no particular reason took it out of the ashcan and dropped it into the mailbox. The gesture would be something to tell Caryl.

He shivered in the unnatural cold as he crossed the Cambridge Common.

THE INNOCENTS

In 1963 many of the girls were Mia Farrow, who looked out at them Monday and Wednesday from their television screens; she did not look out at them on Friday because she was doing something else on Friday and because all the girls were at the record hop.

Mia Farrow had long blond hair and a startled expression. It was a kind of beauty that flourishes in Hollywood and other tropical islands, so Henry McLeod told his English class one Friday, and that night his comment was repeated at thirty-three dinner tables, and at a thirty-fourth, where Elizabeth Anne listened enthralled. Elizabeth Anne Scroyne, a younger and less purposeful edition of Mrs. Elizabeth Anne Scroyne, had black hair and an excess of puppy fat, but she wore her hair long and looked constantly startled and thus presumed that she also was Mia Farrow. Later, at the dance, she kept an eye out for Henry McLeod. Her mother, she knew, had him cornered.

"Don't the girls look lovely," Mrs. Scroyne said.

"They all look like that girl on television."

"Mia Farrow, you mean."

"Yes, Mia Farrow. She has that Vermont kind of beauty that flourishes . . ."

"Well, I don't know I'd say that."

Mrs. Scroyne thought about the things she would say, her own personal opinions, if she could speak to this McLeod straight out. About George flunking English, which was McLeod's fault. About

Elizabeth Anne's diary, discovered this morning, which was probably McLeod's fault too. About how hard it is to prefect the record hop when you're watching your weight and your husband is only a plumber and you have to be nice to people like the Thomasites who have never had a worry in their lives because they're educated and come from rich families that don't worry about insurance payments on the car or . . . She looked up to find McLeod staring at her blankly.

"I don't know I'd say that at all," she continued. "But you look with a different eye, Father McLeod. I mean, you do, don't you?"

"Mr. McLeod." He corrected her and smiled politely. "I'm not ordained yet. Mister."

"Father is a mark of respect. I always want the children to call you Father. All the Thomasites. Which is what I mean when I say you see things with a different eye. You're for the priesthood."

Mrs. Scroyne had more to say but, since Mrs. Sullivan was bearing down on them, she had to content herself with looking at him in a way that meant she knew much more than she was saying. The look was not lost on Mrs. Sullivan, though it meant nothing to Henry McLeod, who sighed and stirred his muddy coffee with a cardboard spoon.

This was the worst part of prefecting the record hops: the half-hour coffee breaks with the Mothers Club.

* * *

"I will see Hank tomorrow night at the hop and he will hold me in his arms and smother me with hot kisses."

Elizabeth Anne Scroyne had first written "with smothering kisses," but with an eye for style she had crossed out the "smothering" and substituted "hot." Because her diary was about Hank, it mattered to her that it be well written, even though nobody would ever read it except, perhaps someday, Hank himself.

Mrs. Scroyne, reading her daughter's diary, frowned and pursed her lips. George's influence, she thought. It distressed her that her children confided more in each other than in her, though she was mistaken; neither confided in anyone. She read on.

" 'Oh, my darling, my darling,' he will wisper tenderly in my ears as I feel his brutal body crushing itself against my soft womanly flesh. He will run his hands through my long silky hair and bury his face in its sweet perfumes, wispering 'Oh, my darling, my darling.' I will say, 'No, Hank, not here. I will give myself to you only when the right time has come.' 'Now, now,' he will respond. 'It cannot be,' I will respond. And in response, he will crush me to him and smother me with hot kisses, wispering . . ."

The passage ran on to the next page, but Mrs. Scroyne skipped the several hot kisses that followed and went directly to the end, where she was not surprised to discover her daughter's virginity still intact and Hank, whoever he might be, still crushing and whispering.

She frowned again, and with the book in her hand lowered her considerable bulk into her daughter's chair. She liked this bedroom despite the photos of the Beatles and Roy Orbison and a poster for "Beach Blanket Bingo." She liked the way Elizabeth Anne kept it neat—compensation for her weight problem, no doubt— but it was important for fat girls to be especially neat. She opened the diary to the last entry and read it through once more. Well, at any rate, her daughter was a good writer, thank God for small favors.

Elizabeth Anne, a freshman at the public high school, had always done well in class. George was the problem. Mrs. Scroyne had decided to take him out of the public school after eighth grade. It would be good for him to get trained by the Thomasites and besides, she reasoned, Albert could do overtime whenever Acme Plumbing had some for him, so they could handle the financial end. George, by God, was not going to turn out to be a plumber, not if she had anything to say about it.

Accordingly George was sent to the local private school taught by the Thomasite Fathers where, despite their assurance that he was bright and promising, he had for three years received only mediocre marks. For three years, that is, until this year, when Mr. Henry McLeod had given him a D in the first marking period and an F in the second. The D, F pattern had repeated itself in the next two periods, until now George's passing or flunking depended wholly on his next and final mark.

Mrs. Scroyne shifted uneasily in the chair. If only George had some of Elizabeth Anne's writing ability. Though, to be fair, the problem was not so much his as that damned McLeod's. He marked much too hard and expected too much of the boys. Symbols, he talked about, imagine.

She flipped to the first entry in the diary. There was no indication there of who Hank was, if indeed there was a Hank. Elizabeth Anne watched too much television—"Peyton Place," for instance —and was at that age when girls exaggerate about romance. They invent, Mrs. Scroyne told herself, especially when they're not pretty. She leafed through the diary, her eyes sharp for the name Hank, her lips curved in a slight smile as she recalled that she herself had been very pretty as a girl.

"I will call him Hank," she read, "even although his name is Henry. He is a priest but not really, that is, he is going to be a priest but he is not yet ordained a priest and I asked him if that meant he could leave someday and get married. He said *yes!* He is very tall (six feet two) with dreamy eyes that are as blue as the sky. His teeth are like the pearl on my mother-of-pearl plastic mirror and very straight. He is very blond and blue-eyed and just like Paul Newman, only even handsomer. George has him in class and says he is O.K. but a hard marker. I think he is the coolest boy I have ever seen in my entire life, and Mary Ellen who has been going to the dances for a whole year says that once they prefect they have to prefect all the time. So I will be seeing *plenty* of him. It is now quarter to one in the A.M. and time for bed. All my homework is done."

Though the entry continued, Mrs. Scroyne did not. Jesus, Mary, and Joseph, she said to herself, Hank is that damned Mc-Leod. She checked the date of the entry—October 5, 1962—and was astounded that this could have gone on for, what, eight months under her own personal eyes and she none the wiser.

How little we know our own children, she thought, turning pages rapidly now, looking for further entries about Hank. A girl-hood crush. Puppy love. She wondered if Henry McLeod knew about this. He must. Suddenly the thought struck her that perhaps Elizabeth Anne had said something to him and that explained George's marks. Tonight at the record hop she must keep her eyes on McLeod. She lit upon another entry.

"I have bought him a beautiful wallet which I think is a very appropriate gift for Christmas for a priest. It is made of *genuine* pin seal and it comes from Italy, even although it has been made by the London Harness Co. of England. It is an imported wallet with a flap to hide your name and your pictures. It cost me twelve dollars and ninety-five cents ($12.95), plus tax, and it is black. I will present it to him at the Friday hop when no one else is around."

Mrs. Scroyne skipped the following four entries and concentrated on Friday.

"I lost my courage to give it to him in person but I was clever enough to sneak into the Mothers Club room and pretend to ask Ma to borrow her comb because I had forgotten mine. While I was there I slipped it into his coat pocket where he will find it. He always leaves his coat on the windowsill, which I know from watching what he does with his coat now that winter is upon us. I love him with all my heart and will never love anyone else. Happy Christmas to all and to all a good night."

Mrs. Scroyne decided she badly needed a cup of tea. She had been wise, she felt, never to trust her children too far. Periodic raids on their bureau drawers and closets had kept her in touch with the underside of their lives, about which she forced herself to keep silence. The knowledge was enough for her. The most difficult silence she had kept was after she found a package of contraceptives hidden in George's football helmet. A week's watching told her he was probably not guilty. A monthly check of his room assured her that since the package still contained the three rubber tubes, it was probably just boyish showing off. Her worries were groundless; George was still a virgin.

In fact, her fears were as ill-timed as her relief, since George had lost his virginity a full year earlier; the contraceptives had been an afterthought, and he kept them on hand against some future opportunity.

His mother, however, enjoyed once more her sense of reprieve as she finished her cup of tea this Friday morning. She poured herself another before returning to the diary.

"Hank is the kind of man"—it was March now and Henry Mc-
Leod had become a man, Elizabeth Anne a woman—"who ad-
mires a woman because she is a person first, even although she
might not be a raveing beauty. We discussed these matters at tonight's hop. He is very mature and I think he realizes that my
love for him is also mature."

Mature, she said to herself, mature. And she flicked the pages
over angrily. By early April, she noticed, there was a growing in-
tensity in their relations, with a great deal of talk about his strong
young arms and her soft breasts. Soft breasts indeed. Thinking
back, though, Elizabeth Anne had been looking, well, less fat
lately. And eating less too. Sure enough, late April announced
that she had lost nine pounds. Once more succeeding entries
dwelt on the shape and the fullness of her breasts.

Of course McLeod was handsome, it's true. That was why she
noticed him in the first place. In each group of unordained
Thomasites there was always one who was good-looking, "one
stud," she had caught herself thinking when she first met Henry
McLeod. It was too bad he was such a bastard about George's
marks. Brilliant, no doubt, since everybody said it, but deep down
the kind that would leave and get married in a year or so. He had a
roving eye, or some kind of eye; anyway, he saw things differ-
ently from the others.

Mrs. Scroyne leafed through May, annoyed at the soft breasts
and the shared maturity of their love and the generally rapid advance of Elizabeth Anne's imaginings. If they were imaginings.
But of course they had to be. She was hopelessly shy, and he
was far too careful. Careful wasn't the question; that he would
even look at a girl like Elizabeth Anne was ridiculous. Ridiculous.
Tonight at the hop she would watch him, she would drop hints,
give him looks. By God, she would get to the bottom of this.

She finished the diary and closed it with a thump as if she were
punishing it. How had she missed it all these months? Elizabeth
Anne must shift hiding places. Frowning still, Mrs. Scroyne returned the diary to its nest beneath the Kleenex. Clever of her,
she thought, to cover it with Kleenex.

When Elizabeth Anne returned from school, her sandwich was
ready on the kitchen counter and her mother was unusually

pleasant to her, so much so that the girl went immediately to check her diary, but that was safe exactly as she had left it. Still, with Ma you could never be sure.

Later, at the dinner table, George told them all what McLeod had said about Mia Farrow in class that day. Mr. Scroyne chewed the stringy roast and Mrs. Scroyne chewed on her lip, her head cocked to one side in judgment. But Elizabeth Anne listened enthralled, because tonight was to be the night of nights with her beloved Hank.

* * *

"I guess you don't enjoy dances, Mr. McLeod. I guess you'd rather be over there in your room reading and studying." Mrs. Sullivan, all bones and nerves and dyed yellow hair, bore down on them, talking as she came.

"As a matter of fact, I would."

"Of course he would. He's like my George. You just can't tear George away from his books, at least ever since he's had Father in class." Mrs. Scroyne shot him an approving smile.

"My Timmy used to like books, but not any more. The way they tear them apart these days ruins all the enjoyment. You don't enjoy something like that." Timmy Sullivan, like George, was in danger of flunking Mr. McLeod's English course, but for Timmy, disaster was certain. Mrs. Sullivan knew this and felt she had nothing to lose by putting Skinnamalink McLeod, as she called him, straight in his place.

"They do. They tear them apart," Mrs. Scroyne said, her loyalties wavering for a moment. "It helps them understand, though. Now, take George. He loves school. I did too. I always was a great lover of school. And just like here, we had the good teachers. Parochial."

"I didn't. I hated school all the time."

"I loved my school." Mrs. Scroyne shook her head, evidently in dismay at such early folly.

"I hated it. I couldn't wait to quit, I was so anxious. But it was different, you know, not like now." Her voice grew less petulant, thoughtful almost, and she tilted her yellow head to one side like a reflective chicken. "It was during the war and all the teachers joined up, the patriotic ones, and you had the beginners, the student teachers, who were only a couple of years older than yourself and they followed the book to see what next."

"I know what you mean. The war. I was lucky to have the parochial. They taught us all the marks of respect as well as good literature."

Silent and miserable, Henry McLeod sat between the two women waiting for the coffee break to end.

Mrs. Sullivan remained lost in reverie. "Those were the days before your time, Mr. McLeod, when all the boys were going off to war and everybody was going into war work, there was plenty of cash in the machine shops and everything, and the boys were getting furloughs and everything was mixed up. That was the big problem, really, if you diagnosed it. Everything was mixed up. It was all the war. Sure, the war." Mr. McLeod made a movement as if to rise. "So I appreciate the need of a good education for my children. Believe me, I know."

"So do I," Mrs. Scroyne said. "We had really good teachers and they taught us the literature. We got the story and the characters down. We didn't have any of this symbolism stuff that was above us. That's all too complicated for teen-agers, if you ask my own personal opinion."

"Excuse me, Mrs. Scroyne, Mrs. Sullivan. I'd better look in on the dance." Henry McLeod rose to leave and felt for the second time his arm brushing against Mrs. Scroyne's immense bosom, which for some reason she had slung across the desk like a sack of laundry. He recoiled, thinking for a moment she had brushed against him intentionally.

"Well, it was lovely, Mr. McLeod."

"Yes, it was lovely, Father." And before Mrs. Sullivan could say it, Mrs. Scroyne did. "That one makes me sick, just sick. But at least I put him in his place."

"*I* put him in his place." Her yellow head bobbed and her eyes narrowed to thin slits. "I was the one who said straight to him that I hated school."

"You were speaking only about yourself. I gave examples of

how it should be done, teaching, and what the trouble is with his classes. Symbols, imagine, at sixteen and seventeen."

"Some of the things they read I just don't approve of. But I've got my eye on him. He looks like the kind that might assign *Catcher in the Rye* before the year is over, and if he does, I'm going straight to the principal."

Mrs. Scroyne had never heard of *Catcher in the Rye*, but she narrowed her eyes like Mrs. Sullivan's and said, "So am I. Straight to the principal with my own personal objections."

It was a standoff.

"Coffee?"

"No, not for me. Well, I might as well. And bring one of your fig squares, I'll just nibble one. Then I'll help in the Ladies."

* * *

The Friday night record hop, a source of embarrassment and dismay to Henry McLeod, was a source of considerable revenue to the school's officials, and therefore attendance as prefects was urged upon all the Thomasites who were priests and made obligatory for all those who were not.

Over the years conduct at the dance had become almost ceremonial for both prefects and dancers. Boys and girls formed long and separate lines, boys to the right and girls to the left, paid their seventy-five cents, and were admitted to the gymnasium proper. Guarding the door to the right was a Thomasite who checked the boys for duck-tailed haircuts, long sideburns, liquored breath, string ties or no tie at all, wide belts, tight pants, steel-tapped shoes—any of these defects being sufficient to disqualify the offender from entering. On the left the Mothers Club decided the fate of the girls who, though they had fewer categories in which to fail, were more carefully scrutinized for beehive hairdos, heavy makeup, liquored breath, transparent blouses, risky decolletage, sneakers. This physical examination was conducted before the ticket was purchased. At the ticket desk itself an identification card was shown, checked, and, if it met approval, the ticket was surrendered. The whole process was surprisingly brisk, the examiners and checkers and sellers being expert at their work. Because the rules were well established, few young people were turned away, and they were almost always unattractive anyway, so nobody minded.

Some mothers and many Thomasites were appointed as prefects of the dance floor itself, to watch for possible fights, to catch the idiot who periodically set off firecrackers, to keep the couples from dancing too closely during the often fatal last three dances. No one was sure what "too closely" meant, but Henry McLeod had once told his class that when it looked to the casual observer that the couple might well be having intercourse, upright and swaying to the music, then they were too close. This statement had made him famous in the school and, for a brief while, popular. It had not, however, clarified the meaning of "too closely," and prefects remained in great need toward the end of the evening.

None of the mothers was assigned to the washroom reserved for the girls, but periodically one would stop by for a brief check; drinking among the girls was rare, but there was no limit to the number or the indecency of things they would write on the walls, so spot checks were necessary. Raids, the girls called them. In the boys' washroom, drinking was usually a problem, and there had been one dreadful case of exhibitionism where a young man had tried to make good his boast that he could urinate into a sink from ten feet distant. He succeeded. Immediately a challenger arose, and then another, until very soon nine young men were lined up facing the sinks in an attempt to duplicate the feat. It was at this moment, at full stream, that Father O'Grady stumbled through the door and stood there, confounded, as the vision penetrated his customary alcoholic stupor. He left and never returned to the record hops again, but word of his discovery spread through the school, and since that time the washroom had been guarded against a repetition of the unfortunate incident.

For the most part the Thomasites accepted their prefecting assignments as another tedious job to be gotten through, no more or less irksome than the parish call on Sunday.

For Henry McLeod, however, the hop was something else. He found it irksome and more. The prefecting, the pettiness about details of dress and person, the enormous scaffolding of law that surrounded attendance at the dance, the hypocrisy and backbiting

in the Mothers Club, the suspicion of something violent or cor-
rupting that lurked just beneath the surface of the evening—all
this struck deep in him.

The hop is original sin, he once told himself, but that was an
absurd thought, and he dismissed it without even bothering to
repeat it to his class.

* * *

By the time Henry McLeod had finished his coffee break, the
dance had entered its second phase. The favorite new dances—
the Swim, the Monkey, the Rexicana Romp, the Mashed Potato
—were abandoned for the favorite old dances, which allowed part-
ners to hold each other in their arms. It was one of these, "Moon
River," that boomed from the amplifier as Henry McLeod crossed
by the ticket desk and was spotted by Elizabeth Anne Scroyne,
who stepped back into the crowd and whispered "now" to her
friend and confidante, Mary Ellen.

* * *

Mrs. Scroyne had enjoyed her coffee and fig square; now on her
way for a spot check of the girls' washroom, she was content. It
wasn't the food, that wasn't it at all, she told herself. It was that
she was sure now that Elizabeth Anne had said nothing to
McLeod; he would have revealed something, she'd have seen it
in his eyes. No, Elizabeth Anne was simply imagining things.

Feeling this way, she was not prepared to see her daughter suddenly leave the dance and slip out the door to the parking lot. This
was expressly forbidden, and Elizabeth Anne was not the kind to
disobey. Or was she? She was at that age. And could McLeod
possibly be meeting her out there, not for the hot kisses, of course,
but just to talk to her? Ridiculous. She pushed on into the
washroom, where the more sophisticated were waiting out the
Thomasite Hail Mary that marked the halfway point of the dance.

"The prayer's over, girls," Mrs. Scroyne said, scowling omi-
nously. But her heart wasn't in her work, preoccupied as she was
with Elizabeth Anne and "Hank," and so the girls filed out un-

admonished. Filing out behind them, she was amazed to see Henry McLeod leave the dance and, with a small nod in her direction, slip out the door to the parking lot.

He thinks I don't know, she said to herself, and after a carefully measured two minutes, followed him.

* * *

According to plan, Mary Ellen had approached him as soon as he entered the gymnasium after his coffee break. Mary Ellen's mooning over Henry McLeod was much joked about among the Thomasites; he himself was amused by it, since she was a bright, lively little thing whose chatter provided a distraction during the long evening. She was always accompanied by the fat and startled Elizabeth Anne, who never spoke at all but who seemed like a nice little girl and, God help her, he thought, she has that bitch for a mother.

Mary Ellen skipped up to him. "Excuse me, Mr. McLeod, but one of the priests was looking for you and I said you were having coffee and he asked me to tell you that there's someone to see you in the parking lot."

"Really," he said, confused. "Who is it, Mary Ellen, do you know?"

"He was an older priest," she said, looking away. "He's way down at the front, I think. I don't know his name."

"No, I mean who's here to see me in the parking lot?"

"He didn't say. He just said to tell you."

And so Henry McLeod went to the parking lot, where there was no one except Elizabeth Anne Scroyne, who was fiddling with the buttons of her pale blue sweater.

"Well, hello," he said, surprised to see her alone behind the gymnasium. She clasped her sweater about her and said nothing. "I was looking for a friend, Elizabeth Anne, somebody who wanted to see me. Have you seen anybody?"

"It was me," she whispered.

"Pardon me? Are you feeling all right? What are you doing out here all alone?"

"It was me. I wanted to see you." She was toying with the white collar beneath her sweater, but she would not look at him.

"What is it? What's the matter? Are you sick?"

She turned her face up to him and he was astonished at her eyes, which implored that he would not, like all the others, reject her. She looked as if she were drowning.

He was deeply moved and stood staring into her face even after she had closed her eyes. He was so moved in fact that it was a full minute before he lowered his glance and discovered that Elizabeth Anne was standing before him with her sweater held wide open to reveal her breasts clearly visible beneath her transparent blouse.

Henry McLeod had never seen a woman's breasts, had never allowed himself even to think of them. Now, panic-stricken, he raised his hands to push her away and she, mistaking the gesture, threw herself into his arms whispering, "My darling, my darling."

He extricated himself from her embrace and stormed back to the dance, but not before Mrs. Elizabeth Anne Scroyne had seen everything—the longing look, the breasts, the embrace. She was quiet the rest of the evening, marveling as she often did at how little we know our children.

* * *

"The evening was tragic but beautiful. Hank and I kept away from each other during the first part of the dance to throw people off the track and then, after the prayer, we met in the parking lot, as it is our custom. Summer is almost upon us now, so the night was heavenly with extatic perfumes and merrily twinkling stars. When Hank came to me, it was the full-fillment of *all* our dreams. He held my face between his hands and kissed me tenderly on several occasions, and then he crushed me in his strong young arms (and I let him touch my woman's breasts this time) and we embraced a *lot*. It was a beautiful thing to go through. After, he said he had failed his God because he is fated to be a priest which is the will of God. (I must confess I shed bitter tears!) Therefore I told him we could not meet again because I would not be willing to come between him and God. So I give him up but I will never love another. I will be his forever. It was the most tragic and beautiful night of my whole life. It is a quarter to one in the morning."

When Mrs. Scroyne read this on Monday, she had already put much thought into what must be done. She had no interest in injuring Henry McLeod, and she was unwilling to expose her daughter and herself to the possible ridicule of the Thomasite principal, that grinning bulldog. She had decided therefore to wait. If George passed English, she would do nothing. If he failed, she would go straight to the principal. She imagined a denunciation similar to the excommunication scene in *Becket*, with herself as the saint declaiming from the guilty diary, and the Mothers Club standing around with lighted candles which they would later stump out against the gymnasium floor. But this was something she could not allow herself unless George flunked. The safer path is always the better path, she knew. She would bide her time.

* * *

The time passed and George flunked and Mrs. Scroyne went straight to the principal with her own personal objections. The denunciation was far less dramatic than she had imagined, but in certain ways even more effective.

The implausible diary did nothing to convince the principal that Mr. McLeod, a good teacher though imprudent in speech, was guilty of misconduct. Nor did Mrs. Scroyne's personal observations convince him. But in a brief interview with Henry McLeod himself, an interview conducted in the corridor while students were changing classrooms, the principal discovered that something indeed had happened in the parking lot. That was more than he wanted to know, and he closed the investigation immediately. Scandal would injure the school and permanently discontinue the record hops, a fine, innocent recreation and a major source of income for the school.

The plan of action was clear. George was passed, though on trial, and it was recommended that he take a summer course in English, a recommendation that in his moment of triumph he felt free to ignore.

Mr. Henry McLeod was transferred immediately to another of

the Thomasites' schools, and his ordination to the priesthood was postponed for a year. He was never told why.

Otherwise, everything continued exactly as it always had been. But that was long ago in the summer of 1963, when many of the girls were Mia Farrow and went to record hops on Friday.

SINS OF THOUGHT, SINS OF DESIRE

UNTIL SHE was twenty-six Beezie Connors had never thought of murdering anyone, and by that time she was Sister Mary Thekla, a teacher of English in the Sisters of Divine Prudence.

"I only thought of it, Father. I'm not certain I desired it, but I know I thought of it."

"I see." The words came out "I shee," because Father Rolfe spoke through jaws clenched tight on a yawn. He was tired, and he knew that that young Turk, Snee or Snay or something, had already cozied the ice for drinks.

"I didn't do it, of course."

"No, yes, that's just as well." He gathered himself for speech. "In the spiritual life, Sister, these thoughts come to us—murder, adultery, oh, terrible things—and we resist, Sister, because we are soldiers of Christ, fighting His battles, and He it is who gives us the strength. He is the commander; we are the foot soldiers. He is the chief; we the followers. He is the five-star general; we, uh, you see the point. And so it is, too, in the spiritual life."

What had happened? He'd come full circle. Well, no matter, they were all good girls.

"So never be discouraged, Sister, keep up the fine work for Jesus. Remember, He gives and He takes away." Oh dear, that was another speech. "Grace is everything, Sister; follow the promptings. Always follow the promptings."

So much for that. Another day, another dolor, ho ho ho.

"Now for your penance say three Hail Marys and a Glory Be."

Here he shifted his generous bulk to the left and freed his shorts, which were stuck. He was sweaty all over from that damned leather cushion.

"Ah, yes. May almighty God have mercy on you, forgive you your sins, and . . ."

The monotone mutter began, and Father's right hand swung into action and Sister Thekla left the confessional absolved. The little window rattled shut behind her.

* * *

Sister Thekla had thought of murdering Mother Humiliata, an intransigent nun who bore a startling resemblance to Sophie Tucker and who with ease combined in herself the power of convent Superior and high school principal. She was held in awe by her community not because of her virtue or wisdom but because for eighteen years she had managed always to hold some kind of Superior's position: Sister treasurer, minister of material needs, principal. "Your money, your food, or your life," Sister Thekla said, reminding herself not to be uncharitable. That was in January. By October Mother had become openly hostile, and by November Sister Thekla in a rage, if only for a second, had thought of murdering Big Mama, as she called Reverend Mother.

She had thought of it. And despite her uncertainty in confession, she had desired it. But she had not done it. She had not, though she was capable of it. Hers was a character that finds its natural home in wars and in pure politics and in religious life, for she was one of those single-minded persons who are able to live for an ideal and to die for it, and are able also to kill for it. In this she resembled Mother Humiliata herself and a fair proportion of the Sisters of Divine Prudence.

Stupid of me even to confess it, she thought. As if I could do such a thing. And she went off to Sister Aelred's room for tea, which was forbidden by Holy Rule.

Murder, imagine, Father Rolfe said to himself, and dismissed the matter from his mind. Good old Snee would have the scotch ready, thanks be to God and His holy Mother.

And so a month later, when Mother Humiliata was found dead, pinioned to her seat by the steering wheel of house car No. 2, it surprised Father Sneigh—age twenty-nine and of a naturally nervous disposition—to learn in confession that Father Rolfe felt himself guilty of criminal negligence in the matter of Mother's death and that Sister Thekla, normally a sensible girl, suspected Mother might have committed suicide.

* * *

But that was a month away, and at the moment Sister Thekla, newly absolved, was saying to Sister Aelred, "You know, Aelred, I think old Rolfe's going bonkers."

"But he's always been bonkers. That's how he is."

"I know, but this is different. Tonight he started giving me the 'so too in the spiritual life' speech, and then he got off onto the five-star general and then, of all things, the death of a relative speech, and then back to 'so too in the spiritual life.' "

"You put your own sugar in. You always want something different when I do it."

"Big Mama."

"Big Mama."

They toasted Mother Humiliata, clinked their tea cups together, and drank, glad that theirs was a holy conspiracy.

In the newest section of the convent Father Sneigh gave his watch an angry glance. Five to nine; old Rolfe would be hulking in any minute for his two or three nightcaps and his predictions of evil days. Father Sneigh did not mind the nightly visits—it was company of a sort—but they always fell right in the middle of his studies. For years he had been working on exegesis of the Kurios passage from Philippians, but how could you ever get going if you were being interrupted all the time. How could you sift your notes. How . . .

There was a knock, and in hulked Father Rolfe.

"Another day, another dolor, ho ho ho."

That again, he thought, and filled the glasses, responding automatically, "Ho ho ho." It was not laughter but gentle self-mockery; it was what passed for a sense of humor in Father Rolfe.

"Your health, Snay."

"Sneigh. As in sky."

"Your health all the same."

Drop dead, Father Sneigh thought, and surprised himself, for he did not have a whimsical turn of mind.

In the oldest section of the convent Mother Humiliata sat holding the autobiography of the Little Flower, a saint to whom she had special devotion. She held the book tilted toward the lamp, with its sixty-watt bulb. Though the other nuns were allowed only a forty-watt bulb, Mother justified her extra twenty watts on the grounds that she was a Superior and could not afford to risk eyestrain. At the moment there was no danger of eye or any other strain, since Mother had fallen gently asleep just as the Little Flower was receiving "the miracle of the snows" she had requested, a snowfall Mother would have found less remarkable had she known that the miracle occurred in the dead of winter.

* * *

Relations between Sister Thekla and Mother Humiliata had been strained from the start. On her way from her previous assignment at the rather too liberal St. Weston's, Sister had stopped to visit her parents, and while visiting was not actually forbidden, it was certainly not done until after final vows. Her arrival at Our Lady of Prudence High coincided with an epic downpour, and Sister, shrouded in a flamboyant yellow slicker, dashed back and forth between the car and the portico carrying more books than any nun was allowed to possess. Mother had noted these things and would note others.

Sister's real troubles began during the time for manifestation of conscience, a twice annual event in which each Sister was summoned by Mother Superior, so Holy Rule said, "for the purpose of revealing herself with all her shortcomings and failures honestly and completely numbered so that the Superior may command whatever measures she thinks good for the spiritual amelioration of the Sister and the edification of the community."

"It means you get what's coming to you," Thekla said.

"If only things didn't upset her so much."

"What things?"

"You can never tell till after she's upset."

"It's when her face goes puce that I worry."

Mother Humiliata looked upon manifestations as the most trying time of a life spent in unremitting trial. Someone always said something upsetting. This time it was Sister Annunciata who, cross-examined for the third time, admitted that when she made the rounds with the morning "Deo gratias," Sister Thekla was nearly an hour late rising. Her testimony was made worse by Sister Maudita's admission, again under examination, that she frequently had evening tea in Sister Aelred's room along with Sister Thekla. The three of them, the unholy trinity, Mother thought. Nor did it help Sister Thekla's case that on the day before her interview she drove house car No. 2 into an evergreen on the front lawn for the sum of four hundred dollars' damage.

The accident had happened, so Sister Thekla claimed, because the steering wheel had locked in place and something funny had gone wrong with the accelerator. Moreover, when she tried to turn off the ignition, the key had simply stuck where it was. Whatever the facts, Mother Humiliata was not pleased.

Sister Thekla's manifestation at first went smoothly enough. She managed to confess faults that were genuine—moodiness, distractions in prayer, occasional negligence in preparing classes —without having to get onto more uncomfortable ground. She had steered clear of the sleeping business and the tea. Manifestation seemed to be gliding to a penance, a blessing, and a dismissal, when suddenly Mother Humiliata smacked her meaty palm against the desktop.

"And these books? What about these books?"

"Books, Reverend Mother?"

"Reports have been made, Sister. Charges have been brought."

"I'm afraid I don't under . . ."

"Tennessee Williams, Sister; does that ring a bell? Graham Greene? Faulkner?" Her voice rose in volume and pitch as she ticked off the offending names. "*Catcher in the Rye*, Sister? Evelyn Waugh? Steinbeck?" On Steinbeck, Mother's face began to turn puce.

"Of those writers, Reverend Mother, I've taught only Steinbeck's *The Pearl*, and that's . . ."

"You admit it!"

"It's on the required reading list."

"I thought you'd have some sort of explanation like that, Sister. Well, let me tell you right now."

Mother Humiliata told her right then, and proceeded for a half hour to tell her a great deal more, about books and tea and sleeping. She was furious with a holy fury, not at Sister Thekla herself, but at the very idea that there were always people in this world who made the smooth ordering of existence impossible. Her rage was impersonal; Sister Thekla merely provided the occasion.

"You are preparing for final vows, Sister Thekla. I want you in the coming months to think hard about whether or not you belong in the religious life. *I* think not. And I promise you, unless you rise at the appointed hour and not a minute later, you will last in the Sisters of Divine Prudence just as long as it takes me to write a letter to Rome. Now get out."

And Sister Thekla got out, murder in her mind.

At once she went looking for Sister Aelred and found her with Sister Maudita, who was crying because Mother had threatened to postpone her final vows for a year.

"Why?"

"The tea. The damned tea."

"How many years did you get, Aelred?"

"None. I told her I was thinking of leaving, and that broke her stride."

"She said she would throw me out." Sister Thekla was surprised to hear her voice crack.

"For tea? She can't throw you out just for tea."

"For not getting up."

They all cried for a little while about that, because not getting up *would* be grounds for dismissal. Then it was time for Sisters Aelred and Maudita to help with preparing dinner, their weekly extra. Left alone, Sister Thekla's fighting spirits collapsed, and she spent the rest of the afternoon in chapel wondering if Mother was right and praying she was not. That night in confession she mentioned that for a minute she had thought of committing murder and perhaps had even desired it. But she had not done it.

* * *

Mother Humiliata was killed on December 6, two weeks after the death of President Kennedy. Though deeply moved by the assassination, Mother said that life was for the living and must go on. Accordingly she refused to close school during the days of mourning and permitted her community to watch for an hour each evening the vast television coverage of the wake and burial of the President. Classes were held, duties were performed, life went on.

Sister Thekla, according to holy obedience, met with her regular classes but refused to teach them; nor could she have done so even if she wanted, overwhelmed as she was by the tangible grief, the moral inertia, that seemed to be everywhere. When she went to meet her Adult Christian Doctrine group on Tuesday evening, she was not surprised to find that only two people had come. And when they proposed driving into Washington to stand with that endless line filing past the casket, this struck her as the only sensible action to take.

And so it happened that much of the world and most of the Sisters of Divine Prudence saw on television the Sisters Thekla and Aelred and Maudita, who should have been within the convent walls at work or at prayer. Mother Humiliata, puce colored before the screen, vowed instant vengeance, a vow she retracted within the next few minutes when three of the school's most generous benefactors phoned to congratulate her on sending a delegation of Sisters to the President's wake.

"I felt I must," she said. "I felt I had no choice," and her voice was sad as she spoke at least half the truth. But to herself she said, "Well, there's still her final vows, and she'll take those over my dead body."

Her dead body was found in house car No. 2. The blame for her death was officially laid to the car—the steering wheel and accelerator, to be exact—though Father Rolfe felt he was more than partly to blame, and Sister Thekla harbored suspicions about Mother herself. The cause of greatest wonder in the convent, however, was how Mother Humiliata came to be in a house car in the first place.

Our Lady of Prudence High was the legal owner of three cars: two 1960 Chevrolets, which were known as house car No. 1 and house car No. 2, and a 1963 Oldsmobile, known as the Prisoner of Love. Black and slightly battered, the house cars were kept in the small garage behind the school while the Prisoner of Love, polished daily by old Ralph the handyman, stood gleaming in the oval drive directly beneath Mother's window.

The thirty teaching Sisters in the convent kept the two cars in almost constant use for courses at Catholic University, lectures at Loyola and Woodstock, dentist appointments, doctor appointments, and one daily trip to the psychiatrist. Mother Humiliata approved of none of this, agreeing with the Fates—as her consultants were known—that a Sister without final vows should not be allowed outside the convent walls, whatever the reason. But though she did not approve, she could do nothing to prevent these excursions, since they had the approval of Mother General, who was too much influenced, she felt, by those Jesuits now at the Council. And so to make the cars available to all and to guarantee that no one but herself drove the Oldsmobile, Mother Humiliata ruled that anyone might use either car provided she signed up for it ahead of time.

There were only two forbidden periods when a car was not available: every Friday evening house car No. 2 had to pick up Father Rolfe at St. Ursula's, where he heard the confessions of the retired nuns; every morning from seven till ten house car No. 1 was out, reason unspecified. The reason was not specified because nobody was supposed to know that Sister Dymphna packed off each morning to a psychiatrist, where she made up for her years of convent silence with a marathon hour of talk to Dr. Conroy, whom she loved and feared, and once, shamefully, dreamed about. All the Sisters knew about poor crazy Dymphna, of course, but because it was supposed to be secret, everyone pretended not to.

Mother Humiliata often explained to the Fates that her own

car was always available for emergencies. The only emergency that had ever arisen, however, was during the annual visitation of Mother General, who had insisted on driving one of her Jesuits to the airport in the Oldsmobile. Its other use was for Mother Humiliata's daily trip to the post office, an act of humility she combined with a pleasant drive through the Maryland farm country, and for her Saturday morning visit to her doctor.

For the past eighteen years Mother had risen each Saturday morning, meditated for an hour, attended Mass, breakfasted, and driven off for her treatment. She had found this ritual unpleasant at first, but over the years had come to enjoy it. The embarrassing part lasted only a minute or two, and then there was the long, pleasant talk with the doctor, little Tommy Murphy, who lisped and pouted like an old woman, but who over the years had shown great understanding of the burdens she had to bear as a religious Superior. She never mentioned even to the Fates the nature of her illness, nor did they ask, because they knew it was a delicate matter and they knew too that Mother often had trouble sitting for very long.

* * *

On the final morning of her life Mother Humiliata happened to be in house car No. 2 because on the previous evening she had succumbed for a moment to her ancient vice of eavesdropping. She had passed by the study room after recreation when she heard Sister Maudita's complaining voice and, telling herself she was not going to eavesdrop, not really, she walked back to the door and stood there listening.

". . . yes, with Porkers," she heard Maudita say. "Can you imagine driving all the way to Boston with Porkers? And in that deathtrap too."

Though Mother Humiliata was ignorant of most of the convent nicknames—her own Big Mama would have brought on a monu-mental rage—she knew at once that Maudita was talking about the unfortunate Sister Porcella, and in a way she sympathized with her. She knew, because she herself had told Sister Maudita she might drive to Boston on Saturday for her uncle's funeral; she might also deliver to Mother General the written reports on the manifestations of conscience, and she might also take Sister Porcella, who was deaf, to the Leahy Clinic, where a number of fine doctors were waiting to look into her ears. And in a way she sympathized with Maudita because Sister Porcella, besides being deaf, was a deadly bore, who talked endlessly about her brother the priest who had gone mad from giving his food to starving children during World War I, when in fact everyone knew that he had run off with a floozy who was reputed to be a nightclub singer and was probably something worse.

Having eavesdropped, Mother went to her room furious, not at what she had heard but at what she had done. None of her other failings distressed her in the least, but this one was so beneath her, so embarrassing to confess, that remorse invariably descended on her almost at once. She prescribed for herself a stinging penance, one the Little Flower would have approved. She sent for Sister Thekla.

"You will tell Sister Maudita that you, not she, will pick up Father Rolfe at St. Ursula's tonight; she has my permission to retire early."

"But Reverend Mother . . ."

"And you will tell her that tomorrow she may drive the Oldsmobile to Boston. I will use the house car for my doctor's appointment."

"But Reverend Mother . . ."

"That will be all, Sister Thekla."

As obedience required, Sister Thekla picked up Father Rolfe. Together they drove down the road and eventually drove off the road and across an open field, the car gathering momentum and shooting straight ahead as once again the steering wheel locked. In a panic Sister Thekla thumped at the brake with no effect whatsoever and then, confused, pressed heavily on the accelerator. Perversely, that gave her control of the car once more, and she was able to stop it and then turn it so that once more it pointed toward the road. Only when she had done this, after much fiddling with the gas pedal and the steering wheel, did she allow herself to get hysterical. For five minutes she screamed and cried, making a great deal of noise in the wintry countryside and making Father

Rolfe far more upset than he had been by the wild drive through the field.

She stopped crying finally when Father leaped out of the car and, frantic, began to call for help. She got him back into the car and, having coaxed from him the promise that he personally would explain to Mother what had happened, she drove very slowly along the narrow winding road that brought them after almost an hour to the convent.

Father Rolfe was too unnerved to see Mother immediately, so he stopped to have a drink with Father Sneigh, who was not in. Father helped himself to some scotch anyway, thinking that Sneigh would be along shortly, and then some more scotch, because Sneigh had not come, and after another—a nightcap—he went to bed, still unnerved but no longer recalling why.

Sister Thekla lay sleepless for over an hour, and then decided to write Reverend Mother a note about the car. Mother Humiliata was convinced that there was nothing wrong with it, having twice been assured by old Ralph that the car was in perfect condition, and Thekla feared that with her heavy foot and mighty self-confidence Mother would drive off and kill herself. She slipped the note under Mother's door and returned to bed.

After another sleepless hour, this one spent thinking about *Tess of the D'Urbervilles* and the built-in perils of putting notes under doors, Sister Thekla threw her coat over her nightgown and trudged down to the garage, where she slipped another note under the windshield wiper. "And that takes care of Big Mama," she said. Sister Thekla slept very late the next morning.

* * *

Early the next morning Mother Humiliata woke, appalled to think that her car had gone off to Boston, alone, so to speak. She was consoled, however, that it was the kind of generous action that wiped her slate clean, and that she was once again squared away with her Maker, slates and squares being much to the fore when she contemplated her relations with God. As she dressed she turned over in her mind the topic of this morning's meditation, a tranquil spirit in a troubled world. Before she left for chapel she picked up the note at her door and, with a glance at Thekla's bold handwriting, placed it in the center of her desk. Nothing was so important that it could not wait until after prayer.

Later when Sister Thekla heard about the accident, she went to Mother's room and found her note, unfolded, in the center of the desk. Wondering, she checked the garage and then the car, but could not find the second note. It turned up in Mother's coat pocket. Sister Thekla went off to confer with Father Rolfe, but he had come completely undone, and she could not make him understand that Mother *had* been warned about the dangerous steering wheel, warned not once but twice. It was futile trying to talk sense to him. She spent the rest of the day in prayer, and that night under the seal of confession discussed the matter with Father Sneigh.

How could Mother possibly have driven that car after reading the two notes unless, God forbid, the accident was not an accident? How, she wanted to know.

Father Sneigh, reeling from an hour's session with the distraught Father Rolfe, was confused by Sister Thekla's curious story. He was a Scripture scholar, not a detective; why did these people torture themselves over nothing? The woman was dead, let her rest in peace. She was a dreadful woman anyway.

And so, as soon as he was decently able, Father Sneigh raised his hand in blessing and dismissed Sister Thekla, who would simply have to get along as best she could, relying, like Rolfe and in Rolfe's own formula, on the tender mercies of God and His holy Mother.

Never having grasped her question, Father Sneigh could offer Sister Thekla no answer. The answer was simple: Mother Humiliata had not read either note.

Like any inveterate eavesdropper, Mother was possessed of an insatiable curiosity. But she was curious about only those things she was not supposed to know. Letters from Mother General, official papers that came across her desk, the notes beneath her door held no interest whatsoever for her. If anything, she regarded them with fear and suspicion; a letter from a higher superior meant another departure from ancient custom, and a note from a subject meant a request. Either way, the serene order of convent life was interrupted, so when she saw the note beneath the windshield wiper, she plucked it out and with a glance at the handwriting thrust the bit of paper into her pocket.

"So much for Thekla," she said and, a tranquil spirit in a troubled world, she backed the car smoothly out of the garage.

The morning was cold and clear, and Mother Humiliata drove along the winding road humming "O Sacrament Most Holy." Despite the recent heavy snowfall there was very little snow on the ground, and with the clear air it was a perfect day for driving. Mother began to plan a little excursion for the afternoon, a drive up the Potomac perhaps. When she came to the stretch of road that had been newly paved in late summer, she speeded up a bit. She was not strictly within the speed limit, but there was no traffic on a Saturday morning, and besides, the road was wider here and not nearly so winding.

Her thinking was quite correct. The road was not winding; it was in fact so very nearly straight that she was unaware the steering wheel had locked until she tried to turn the car around a slight bend. Mother slammed her foot on the brake, which did no good at all, and the car shot off the road and into a long gully. It lurched a little and tore off in a new direction. Mother's foot crunched the brake pedal and her eyes bugged as the car gathered more speed, flattening several rows of icy cornstalks and making a neat passage between two enormous oak trees.

It was rather exhilarating, actually.

Beyond the trees another gully and then another field. And in the middle of the field, a cow.

Crazily, Mother Humiliata found herself thinking about the cow. What was it doing in the middle of the field? In December. With snow on the ground. And then it was over. The last thing the cow saw was a huge black car bearing down on it, a nun at the wheel, grinning, as if she had intended this all along.

Mother Humiliata took the cow at sixty miles an hour, accelerating even as she struck it.

STILL MORE ON THE NOSE

IT WAS not at all clear that he was dead. He had been lying immobile for days, his eyelids flickering occasionally and his lips sputtering once, whether in prayer or in spasm nobody was sure, but now there seemed to be a new and different inertness about him. Still, it was in no way certain he was dead.

"I think he's dead." Brother McCarthy was certain. He eyed the intravenous bottles warily, but they looked just the same.

"I don't know. He might be dead." Brother Lavelle felt certain the old man was not dead, but everyone knew how Brother McCarthy stood with the Master of Novices, and if few dared disagree with him, most never even thought of it. Brother Lavelle, smarting from recent admonitions about religious decorum, resisted the temptation to scratch his head. "He might be dead."

"Well, we should call somebody if he's dead. We should call somebody *before* he's dead."

"We can't if he's dead. If he's already dead." Frowning, he explored his thin, sandy hair with dirty fingers.

"Of course not, *if* he's already dead. But if he's *not* dead we ought to call somebody before he does it." Brother McCarthy hated stupidity and was particularly annoyed at Brother Lavelle's. It was, he was sure, stupidity masked with a show of patience and reasonableness. He looked at Brother Lavelle and tried to see Jesus there. Surely, he thought, even Jesus . . . and then he caught himself. "I'm going to call somebody."

Still, it was a serious thing to call somebody. There would be a fuss among the novices, and that would annoy Father Master. Father Assistant was out of the question; he would be furious at being called from his work and, even if he were not furious, he would pretend to be, since that was recognized as good discipline for the novices. Father Master was somebody you didn't just call. Rather he called *you*, and it was a bad sign if he did. It meant that some serious defect had been observed in your religious conduct. As for the Rector, no one was exactly sure what he looked like. He passed by the long row of novices three times a day for meals, but of course with their heads bowed it was difficult even for those who had not disciplined the faculty of sight to make him out exactly in a different context. It was known only that he had a funny walk, rather as if he had been wound up somewhere in the attic and had been marched down to the beat of a metronome. He was celebrated for virtues no one had ever specified, but which were presumed as preceding his appointment to office. Turning over these possibilities in his mind, Brother McCarthy flinched a bit, torn between fear and duty. "I'm going to call somebody." He stood by the bed, not calling anybody.

"Who are you going to call?" Brother Lavelle smoothed his hair, guilty. Unconsciously he began to scratch his behind.

"Whom." He pursed his lips. "Excuse me, Brother. It is not my place to admonish you." He reached inside his habit and tugged down one bead on a string pinned there for the purpose of enumerating failures with ease and accuracy. This was his second failure today.

"Who are you going to call?"

"I'm not sure yet. The Rector maybe." He pondered the canonical rightness of this until his more spiritual instincts asserted themselves. He studied the death mask on the pillow. "The Rector certainly, but I think Father would prefer Father Master to assist at his death. Father Master is spiritual."

"But Father Rector is very spiritual." He searched his mind for evidence of this spirituality. "He's Father Rector, isn't he."

"He *is* Rector and he *is* spiritual. But Father Master is Master of Novices. You can only be Master of Novices if you're approved." He was not sure what it meant to be approved, or indeed who did the approving, but he suspected it was a telling argument against Brother Lavelle, and he was right.

"Yes, that's right." He sighed for his stupidity, and he scratched his head.

"It *is* right."

The two novices remained standing there, contemplating the dead or dying old man. That is to say, Brother Lavelle contemplated the old man. Brother McCarthy contemplated Brother Lavelle. Though stupid and unkempt, Brother Lavelle had an infuriating way of dismissing correction as if it were somehow irrelevant. He gave the impression of forgiving you for telling him what, after all, he had to be told if community life were to be livable. How, he wondered, had Brother Lavelle been admitted in the first place? Dirty fingernails always burrowing through his hair. And his clothes always several degrees shabbier than novitiate custom, as if he had confused sloppiness with poverty. Which he probably had. And the slowness of all his reactions. He never caught the point of a joke, always laughed late enough to make the others feel embarrassed. Always . . . but here he reached inside his habit and pulled down another bead. Three failures so far; two for uncharitable talk, one for uncharitable thoughts.

"Who are you going to call?" Brother Lavelle asked. Brother McCarthy was startled for, despite his concentration on the other's defects, Brother Lavelle was not really there for him.

"I think we should wait. Father Master says never to make a decision in haste."

They turned their attention to the bed and were relieved when the old priest suddenly sighed, confirming the wisdom of Father Master and of Brother McCarthy, who was his disciple in the Lord.

Brother McCarthy smiled modestly at his vindication. Without mentioning that he had already said his prescribed rosary for the day, since that might smack of spiritual pride, he suggested that they say the rosary for the rapid recovery of the dying priest. In the end, however, this turned out to be a mistake, since Brother Lavelle was incapable of saying even the rosary intelligently. He had never caught the knack of beginning the "Holy Mary, Mother of God" part simultaneously with his companion's concluding "fruit of thy womb, Jesus." He dragged the responses horribly. He closed his eyes, which was infuriating. There was no getting around it; charity or no charity, Brother Lavelle was hopelessly stupid.

* * *

As it happened, Brother Lavelle was not stupid. He was slow to respond to humor or hijinks. He was sincere and simple. He was pious with a natural piety never destroyed or even altered by his few years in religion or by his many years out of it. But he was not stupid.

It was a strange fact that what had been cultivated as virtues and recognized as signs of vocation before he entered the Thomasites became, once in, stumbling blocks to the perfection that was the common ideal. He never acknowledged this, neither then nor later, believing always that he simply had been unsuited to religious life and was fortunate in finding this out before he took his vows. When in his later years he gave up his very lucrative job as automobile salesman and purchased the agency, which promptly trebled his income, he earmarked a substantial amount of his yearly earnings as gifts to the order. His two sons attended the order's schools, one of them becoming a Thomasite priest, one a doctor who donated a day each week to the care of the order's elderly priests. His daughter became a nun, and later when she married an ex-priest and raised a large happy family, the Thomasites were careful never to mention her to any of the Lavelles, who remained faithful to the girl but could not condone her life of sin.

Brother McCarthy was a different matter. It is true that, despite a general feeling to the contrary, even he recognized that he did not know everything. Still, he gave a passable imitation and, in the environment of the novitiate where an ability to assimilate and reproduce the held truths of the order was accepted as intelligence, Brother McCarthy was thought to be intelligent in the extreme. Furthermore, he had the advantage of being totally humorless. In time therefore he would become a Scripture scholar, endowed with private revelations on matters as diverse as the author of Hebrews and the nature of tomorrow's weather. Every other year he brought out a small, definitive work on a not very

vexed question from Leviticus. The intervening years were devoted to teaching and research. He developed with time a startling independence of superiors and in fact of the order itself,
so much so that among certain of his friends he became known as
"Shit-Shit McCarthy" because, as he often claimed, "he didn't
give two shits what any of them thought." He was from the beginning sexless and omniscient, one seeming the function of the
other—as if knowledge sterilized or in some remarkable way ste-
rility conferred knowledge. And, having seen the folly to which
it leads and the time that it consumes, he had little patience with
love and no curiosity to experience it. His life therefore was never
once disturbed by either sex or love. Scripture was his life, and
he was recognized as an authority in his field.

But all this was many years away from the novitiate and the
dying old man in the infirmary. Brother Lavelle's automobiles
were still unimagined, and Brother McCarthy's scriptural authority unrecognized when the nurse came to relieve them from their
agonized hour of watching.

* * *

Late in the evening—that is, after nine-thirty, when all the
novices were in bed—Father Master made his reflections on the
day. Making reflection, he liked to point out, was different from
reflecting; it emphasized the will and the need for constant vigi-
lance over the imagination. Father Master had a strong will and a
disciplined imagination, and so it gave him particular pleasure to
sit by the window of his darkened room each evening making his
reflections. He would gaze out over the lake, which was soothing,
he said, and which never looked the same, and let sift through his
mind the things he had noted during the day about house discipline, the spiritual growth of the novices, the perennial problems
that harass those who deal with the soul.

Today had been like all the other days; he had seen to that. Yet
there was always the unpredictable. There had been an incident
of talking at breakfast, he had not noticed who, but he presumed
it was Brother Corning, who generally was guilty. He dwelt on
Brother Corning, asking himself what the Holy Spirit would do

about him. Brother Corning was difficult. A brilliant young man in many ways, but dangerous. He did not conform. He did not fit the mold. He was the kind who in a few years would mislead others with his unpleasant ideas. Coming to think of it, he wasn't even a product of a Thomasite school. How did he get in, do you suppose? And why? Brother Corning. What exactly was it that was so wrong about him? Something about his voice or the way he carried himself. He wasn't exactly feminine, that wasn't it, but there was something in that direction, something . . . artistic, that was it. He spent too much time with books and not enough time in chapel. Or on the ball field. He talked strangely too, like an issue of *The New Yorker*—which, to be sure, did have some amusing cartoons, but which set a sophisticated style totally out of place in a religious. And didn't his mother paint? Or was it his father? That could be checked tomorrow or some future tomorrow. The important thing about making reflection was not to be distracted by the immediate or the practical.

Here Father Master suffered a temptation to daydream about the Red Sox and their miraculous—well, perhaps remarkable—recovery in the race for the pennant. The impossible dream might yet be realized, even without the Big C. Old Lonnie was pitching fine, just fine. Team spirit was magnificent. . . . Father Master returned to making his reflections.

The incident at breakfast. Yes, Brother Corning would have to be spoken to. And watched generally. Then the conference on the rules. That had gone well, but of course the rule under consideration had itself been easy to explain. And the two who recited the rule from memory, one in Latin and one in English, had done well. Brothers Bunting and Butler. Good boys, both Thomasite products, though Brother Butler's recitation left something to be desired in enthusiasm. Brother Lavelle, of course, left everything to be desired. That could be tomorrow's reflection.

Tomorrow's conference was the difficult one. "Wrinkles on the forehead, and still more on the nose, are to be avoided as much as possible." Novices always found this funny at first. Later they came to see that the Constitutions, which included this section of ten rules on deportment, had indeed foreseen every possible situation in their religious lives and had provided for it. The rules looked to everything. Didn't the Pope himself say that if he canonized St. Renfrew, the only novice saint of the order, that he would in effect be canonizing the rules? This always impressed the novices, and well might it. The Rules for Deportment were not so significant as the Rules for Rector or the Rules for the Conduct of Schools, but it was always dangerous with novices to indicate that something was not so important as something else. Immediately they would think it was of no importance at all, and then discipline would break down. No. Better simply to emphasize that the wrinkles rule was another example of how the whole man has been provided for in the Thomasites. Wholeness and holiness, an excellent theme.

Father Master allowed himself a moment to bask in the beauty of the lake. The moon made a golden path on the water; you could walk on that path straight into the arms of God. Surely in the face of such overwhelming natural beauty no man could deny God. Father prayed in gratitude for several minutes and then returned to his reflections.

Lunch was fine. No talking. Good modesty of the eyes. At recreation afterward he had heard Brother Corning complaining about the stew. He wasn't complaining actually, he was being amusing and the others were laughing. Well, laughter didn't hurt. Good boyish laughter, hard playing on the ball field, perfect spiritual recollection: these were the things that made the fine Thomasites of tomorrow.

At work period everyone had worked well. Brother Howath had asked permission for a nap. Granted. A sickly boy with bad skin, but very cooperative and very humble. Took good notes at conference and always knew the memory. No mishaps other than the hoe broken by Brother Lavelle. He had been leaning on it, he said, and requested a penance. A hoe is a small matter. But Brother Lavelle. Not to be thought about today; tomorrow. The new group always had to be weeded out; those who didn't discover by themselves that they ought to leave, sometimes had to be encouraged in that direction. Brother Lavelle seemed one of the latter, but there was time, and the Holy Spirit would handle that problem in His own way.

Rosary, afternoon prayer, dinner. That stringy roast beef. Unchewable. What on earth did they do to it in the kitchen? Another cross built into the place, very good for the novices, and good for the rest of us too. And then the evening, uneventful except for that one confession. Masturbation, a terrible vice. Some men never got over it. It was the right thing to ask point blank if he thought he had a vocation. Night prayers. And now the lake with the moon making a golden path. Christ might walk straight across that water. If only the novices could come to a point where they could see Christ in every moment of their lives. They had come here in the first place to leave the world and its worldliness behind them. Why then was it so difficult to show them the self-discipline necessary to live an other-worldly life? If they saw Christ in all the petty annoyances of their day, life would be so easy, so peaceful.

Profoundly grateful that he himself had found Christ and peace in this difficult life, he knelt by his bed for one last act of contrition before sleep. The knock on his door that took him upstairs to old Father McNamy was a false alarm. Brother Haddock, the ancient lay Brother who watched by the bed through the night, lived in terror of death and, unwilling to face it alone, had summoned Father Master without sufficient reason. Father McNamy did not die, but Father Master lost several hours' sleep, so that the next morning's conference on wrinkles was a more difficult one than he had anticipated.

*   *   *

The conference was not a success. It had begun well, with a slow, rambling explanation of Thomasite concern for the whole man, examples of Brother Renfrew and Father Riccotini illustrating how effectively the rules helped us to crucify self, to shed the old Adam, like a withered snakeskin. Father Master rather fancied this metaphor, though in general he felt metaphor better left to others, and he was pleased to note that even Brother Lavelle had the wit to copy it into his "light book," a personal store of helpful religious axioms each novice kept from the day of his entrance.

Because he had progressed smoothly to the rule itself, laughter was minimal. The growing giddiness that always threatened to sweep through the entire novitiate and that sometimes did so during evening litanies subsided altogether with the second reading of the rule, a reading that on previous occasions had pushed the novices quite over the brink of hilarity into a mild hysteria difficult to cope with. The first few times this had happened Father Master was alarmed; with the years he had grown used to it, even to expect it during the time of the Great Retreat or during periods of protracted silence.

This morning, therefore, had looked particularly promising until by some ill luck a housefly lit on his forehead, sat there for a while, and then proceeded to walk across his brow and down the bridge of his nose. It was one of Father Master's self-imposed disciplines to submit to such things. Giving no indication that he felt anything, therefore, he continued his elaborate unfolding of the rule. The novices held their breath, not listening, while the fly paused for a full two minutes, so Brother Corning said, and he had timed it. And then, to the disbelief of some, to the agonized relief of others, Father Master wrinkled his nose and sneezed. The moment of compressed silence exploded into hilarity.

Because he was furious with all of them, Father Master went against himself—going against self was a frequent theme of his in both conference and confession—and declared a sports holiday. That restored order and, in some way he half understood and spiritually savored, restored the balance of things as well.

That afternoon at the ball field nobody mentioned the conference. There were, as it turned out, many safer things to discuss anyway. The fiftieth anniversary of Father McNamy's priesthood was only a week away. A visiting day was in the offing. The pennant was under serious dispute and, though no newspaper ever reached the novices, Brother McCarthy frequently returned from his trips to Father Master's room with ball scores—revealed, it was feared, in moments of weakness or companionship. Actually they were revealed quite purposely; Father Master felt that, though news tended to distract from the spiritual life, news about sports tended to enforce a manly spirit that was healthy. The Red Sox and the Tigers therefore were the names for today's game. There had been some movement toward the Twins, but Brother Mc-

Carthy let it be understood that from his information the Twins were no longer really running up front.

Brother Corning, a Tiger, was desolate in right field. His summer in religious life had not been at all what he expected; surely the Thomasites must sometimes do something besides play baseball and weed that Goddamned corn patch. Brother Corning, admonished about his language on several occasions, cursed privately and sometimes indulged in silent orgies of vulgarity, which later he dutifully confessed.

The sun was blinding, and of course he had no hat. And that idiot McCarthy blobbing the balls across the plate and having them swatted all over hell. He only plays anyhow because the Master likes it. It's a mockery. McCarthy, the old Father Mocker. He smiled, pleased with himself.

"Corning! For Pot's sake, Corning! Catch it!"

Brother Corning raised his glove in time to prevent himself from being struck by the ball. Astonished to see he had caught it, he made no response to the disbelieving laughter and exaggerated cheers that greeted him. He had no idea where to throw the ball, but nobody noticed his bewilderment since the Sox had just made their third out and the Tigers were now at bat.

Brother Corning wandered to the dirt road beside the field, stopping to pick a long strand of yellowing grass, which he thrust between his front teeth. He crossed his eyes to watch his lips make the grass bobble up and down. It was a sweltering day, perfect for swimming, he thought. And here we are loving Jesus by battering hell out of a pack of string wrapped in cowhide. Led by the old Father Mocker.

"That was really great, Brother Corning!" Brother Lavelle was enthusiastic.

"Yes. I'm becoming a better religious every day." He studied Brother Lavelle with idle curiosity. You poor craphead, he thought, you're as out of it here as I am, except you don't even know it. "Do you want to go for a swim, Brother Lavelle?"

"Well, I mean, yes. But can we?" He kicked at a stone with his shabby sneaker. "I mean, aren't we all supposed to play ball, all together?"

"You aren't playing. You're not on either team."

"But you are. So how could we go?"

Brother McCarthy approached, sufficiently attracted by Brother Corning to put up with the stupidities of Brother Lavelle. Brother Corning held for him a fascination he could not explain, though Brother Corning could have told him that what he wanted was not friendship but admiration. Brother Corning was the only one who actively withheld it, and Brother McCarthy would have it at all costs.

"That was a good catch, Brother Corning. We were all surprised." Brother Corning developed a sudden interest in the almost cloudless sky.

"So was I. I hate baseball."

"Father Master says it's very good for community. It brings everyone together and develops charity. That's why he gives us holidays."

Brother Corning was still studying a wisp of cloud. Brother Lavelle was absorbed in fingering a pimple on the back of his neck, his face screwed up in a hundred wrinkles.

"You can play next inning, if you really want, Brother Lavelle." Brother McCarthy was sure that he *would* want; nonetheless, charity urged him on.

"What?"

It was too easy a solution. "Nothing." Charity, striving to reassert itself, was shoved firmly to the back of his conscience. "How are your banners going, Brother Corning?"

Brother Corning, though only a first-year novice, had been put in charge of the banner-making for Father McNamy's anniversary celebration. The appointment was made by Brother McCarthy who, as novice assistant to Father Master, enjoyed such powers and who thought by conferring distinction upon Brother Corning to win his attention at last. He was prompted by the further consideration that Brother Corning was the only novice capable of both conceiving and executing the elaborate display necessary for such a high festival.

His background proved it. Brother Corning's father, even the novices knew, was a famous painter, though not so famous as his son would become. In those later years some insisted that the oddity of a Thomasite priest who exhibited in the best private galleries and who sold his paintings for breathtaking sums had perhaps exaggerated the critical favor lavished upon him. Still, at this time, it was Brother Corning's father who was famous, while his son made banners in the Thomasite novitiate.

"I'm speaking to you, Brother. I asked how the banners are going."

"The banners are swell. All with good words; that's what Brother Corning says. Good words." Brother Lavelle was not allowed to work on the banners but, with his uncomplicated vision, he had a keen appreciation of their strong-lined originality.

"Good words is no way to speak about Sacred Scripture. Anyway, I was asking Brother Corning."

Brother Corning turned his eyes, the pupils thinned to tiny slits of mockery, full upon Brother McCarthy. "For McNamy's apotheosis, you mean."

Brother McCarthy was silent. Never certain when Brother Corning was joking, never certain what the joke was even when he knew Brother Corning was joking, he hesitated before this one.

"What's apotheosis?" Brother Lavelle knew he was missing something.

"His fiftieth. They're going to come get him in a fiery chariot. We can hang the banners on it and have pony rides for the kids and LSD for the grownups."

"That's not a correct use of the word. Apotheosis means becoming God or becoming divine, and you can't use it to mean a liturgical celebration." Brother McCarthy, having decided it was not a joke, felt that things ought to be put right. Brother Corning's irreverent streak sometimes carried him too far. And yet now, corrected, he seemed only amused. That's the trouble with Corning; he always thinks he's so much above you. Even when he's wrong. And now he's off with the clouds again. Damn him.

"Won't it be an awful thing if Father McNamy doesn't live until his fiftieth. He was so holy and everything, I mean. It would be nice if we could all let him know that." No one replied, Brother Corning intent on the cloud, Brother McCarthy intent on Brother Corning. "It would be a shame if he died."

"It wouldn't be a shame. It would be God's will. It would be God's will both for him and for us, so I don't see how you can call it a shame." Brother McCarthy began to wish he hadn't joined them after all.

"We're going swimming. Get your suit, Brother Lavelle. Mine's at the lake. Hurry up."

"You can't." Brother McCarthy, far from indignant, was merely stating a fact.

Brother Lavelle lurched to the chicken wire fence that served for a batter's cage, managing not to trip on the bat or on the low bench where the more accomplished Thomasite novices waited their turn at the plate. His swimsuit, nestled in a little hollow by the fence, was wrapped in a soiled towel swarming with ants. He stopped to brush them off.

"You can't," Brother McCarthy repeated. "First of all, you're on my team. And second of all, we'll all go swimming after we've all played ball."

"You've got plenty of people to replace me in right field, where nothing ever happens anyhow." Someone was shouting for Brother McCarthy, whose turn it was at bat. "And second of all"—he imitated flawlessly, lips pursed, head wagging—"second of all, I'm going." He stood there, staring over Brother McCarthy's head at the sky.

"Brother McCarthy, you're up! Hey, what the pot, Brother McCarthy!" The Tigers were growing impatient.

"You're disobedient, Brother Corning."

"You're a bag of shit, Brother McCarthy."

Without a word Brother McCarthy turned from him and would have stalked magnificently to the batter's box except for Brother Lavelle who, still brushing ants from his towel, blundered into the path of his rage.

Though he swung wildly three times in succession and though the Sox cheered slightly more than was necessary, Brother McCarthy went against self and said nothing. But he was angry with a terrible anger.

* * *

They had been watching clouds now for twenty minutes. Stretched on their backs, with the cold lake water rocking the raft gently, they were more intimately together than was permitted in the novitiate. Shouts came to them off and on from the ball field, but their real world of loneliness and constant strain toward an unrealizable perfection was distant, blessedly distant, Brother Corning thought. He broke the silence.

"You know, back at the ball field I counted twelve animals in only three clouds." He pondered his own statement. "Twelve."

They were silent again, Brother Corning watching the red and blue fish that swam across his closed eyelids, Brother Lavelle enjoying the sun, his mind free of thought or worry. Brother Corning laughed, softly and to himself at first, and then out loud.

"What's so funny?"

"I told Brother McCarthy he was a bag of shit." He continued laughing.

Brother Lavelle smiled, considered the uncharity of the reflection, and stopped. Suddenly he erupted in a laughter that Brother Corning had never heard from him before. It was round and full, rolling up from his belly.

"What are *you* laughing at?" Brother Corning asked.

"I'm laughing because it's true. He *is* a bag of shit."

Their disobedience in going alone to the lake, their shared uncharity about Brother McCarthy, far from leading them on to the further sins Father Master only vaguely imagined and very distantly feared, prompted them rather to an honesty and openness that it was vainly believed the rules inspired. Brother Lavelle for once felt no urge to scratch anything.

"When I grow up, if they let me grow up, do you know what I want to be? I want to be a painter. I want to do a really great Christ. One where evil wears the mask of the commonplace. Where the buildings are split down the center and nobody notices because they're split down the center too. With lots of priests around, looking how . . . not holy . . . looking competent. With fat asses. And a Mary who looks tired, with no beauty at all except what you can't see. Saggy breasts. Wrinkles. A woman who has failed almost everything. Who has survived pain, but just barely survived. Do you know what I mean?"

Brother Lavelle was mesmerized. He had never heard anyone speak like Brother Corning, never dreamed of being spoken to by him any more than he would dream of being spoken to as an equal by Brother McCarthy. There were hierarchies that even Brother Lavelle recognized. Brother Corning, rolling his head to the side, was astonished to see Brother Lavelle's gaze, half surprise, half desire.

"You. What about you? Tell me," Brother Corning said. "I'd really like to know." And he sounded disarmingly sincere.

"Well, you know. I mean. A priest. I'd like to be a priest."

Brother Lavelle blushed slightly but, finding no negative response and feeling somehow more free to express himself than he could ever remember, he plunged ahead. For over five minutes, with a measured concern quite unlike his usual enthusiasm and with astonishing articulateness, he narrated the growth of his vocation and his simple overriding need to be of help to people, to do something for somebody before he died.

"Because I love Jesus in a way I can't explain. I know I'm so damned clumsy and I have pimples and Brother McCarthy thinks I'm stupid, but just the same, I want to be a priest and I know that someday I'll be able to do things for people. Because Jesus is the most important thing and I love him. I really do."

Brother Corning was the only novice who would not have laughed. He lay on his back tracing a giraffe, wondering how anybody ever got to know anybody, when simple crapheads like Lavelle turned out to be so complicated. Touched, he said nothing.

"I guess I don't make much sense."

"You make perfect sense. You're probably the only person here who does." Brother Corning rolled over on his side and looked straight into Brother Lavelle's eyes. "You're very beautiful, do you know that? You're honest and good and I'm very grateful for what you've just told me. This may sound funny, but it's true: we'll always be friends. Thirty years from now, we'll be friends."

It was true. Ian Corning, the Thomasite painter, and Richard Lavelle became and always remained friends. At first to the astonishment of their acquaintances and later to their amusement, the car salesman from Bridgeport would appear at the champagne suppers that invariably inaugurated a Corning show. Later in the evening Father himself, smart in his mute plaid tuxedo, would escort Richard and Cathy Lavelle from painting to painting, listening with grave attention to their pleased responses and with equal attention to their sometimes startling criticisms. The only picture on display in his studio was a group photo; scrawled across the front was "With all our love, Cathy and Richard," and beneath that, "Richard, Jr., Ian, and Mary Beth." When Richard, Jr. entered the Thomasites, he explained to Father Master, who was not pleased with the information, that he had been much influenced by a Father Corning, who was a friend of the family. It was the same Father Corning who asked Ian if he would volunteer one day each week to take care of the old priests of the order. And, though it was never proved, it was Father Corning who presided at the wedding of Mary Beth and her ex-priest, a sinewy and simple French teacher who loved her deeply and made her happy. Father Corning and Richard Lavelle were so transparently devoted to one another that Cathy sometimes said she had married them both and, though this made Father Corning distinctly uneasy, he knew what she meant and loved her for that instead.

They remained friends, it was true. But at the time of Brother Corning's declaration, it sounded merely funny to Brother Lavelle, funny in a way that seemed somehow wrong. Startled, he stood, and said, "I don't know what you're talking about," and then he dived into the water.

Rounding the bathhouse, Brother McCarthy took in the scene: Brother Corning looking anxious on the raft, Brother Lavelle diving into the water and swimming rapidly toward shore. To Brother O'Hara, even though he was captain of the victorious Sox, Brother McCarthy raised his brows and half muttered, half insinuated, "Two alone at the lake. I wonder how long *they'll* last."

That afternoon Father Master was duly informed, and that evening, in His turn, so was the Holy Spirit.

* * *

Less than a week later, two days before his jubilee, Father McNamy died. His death at first caused Father Master consternation; this soon passed, however, when Father O'Malley, who was in charge of the kitchen, informed him it was too late to cancel food preparations, and indeed the delights prepared to honor Father McNamy while alive would do him no less honor on the day of his burial. Consternation ran high among the novices, however, since for them a major part of the celebration was the hanging of banners and streamers and golden wreathes, the Palestrina sung at Mass, the levity that attended all such lavish Thomasite festivals.

Only Brother McCarthy was seriously grieved. It was he who had been sole witness to Father's death. Old Brother Haddock, sensing that Father McNamy's end was at hand, had fled to the corridor and told the first person he met—this happened to be Brother McCarthy—to watch over Father McNamy while he went to pee. He had remained gone for a half hour, during which his charge had come fully conscious, spoken, died, had been thereupon anointed and hastened on toward his burial.

Entering the room, Brother McCarthy was astonished to see the old man's eyes wide open, his hand moving weakly toward the tubes attached to his right arm. Thinking this might well be the type of miracle that graced the novitiate of St. Renfrew, he called for Brother Haddock, who did not come.

"Father McNamy, you're alive," he shouted, as if to assure the priest that he was not yet in paradise. "You're alive for your fiftieth." And he called once more for Brother Haddock.

The old man moved his leathery lips, but not a sound came out. Brother McCarthy stepped closer to the bed, and bent down over the struggling man so that their noses almost touched. He experienced a sudden and terrible awareness of the presence of death. And then the priest, as he had said almost every day of his adult life, said one final time, "I don't give two shits what any of them . . ." and here he expired. To his credit, Brother McCarthy never revealed to anyone the dying words of Father McNamy, though he was questioned by Father Master, who had known Father's early habits and feared them.

Brother McCarthy alone grieved; something was lost to him, something that had nothing to do with his vocation or his certainty of what his life should be. It was a strange kind of innocence that was lost, and he grieved for that. There was an absence now that needed filling.

After the first surprise of Father's death, the novices consoled one another with the evidence that even if Father had lived he would not have been able to enjoy the preparations they had made. And the holiday would still be theirs since, after a funeral, Father Master always granted a sports afternoon on the conviction that death, like all other things, had to be kept in proper perspective. And the feast itself, with the fun of watching the older priests wobble dizzily from the before-dinner drinks to the modest dinner wine. Some said that once at a jubilee dinner one ancient Father had passed out, collapsing face downward in his soup, but this was rumor and never confirmed. So nothing was lost, really, except of course poor old Father McNamy, who was at last released from the burden of his sufferings.

Father Master used the occasion of Father McNamy's death for two conferences: one on the transitoriness of all things, one on Father McNamy as a man who had lived the rule—he had never put himself forward in studies or in the eyes of the world, he was not one of those well-known Thomasites who risked so much by becoming eminent scholars or theologians, he was a man who had done his job by fading into the woodwork. "He was one of the long black line winding across the sea of this life into the arms of God." Brother Corning had smiled, but the others had been impressed. Brother Corning had been watched and found wanting.

* * *

Early in the morning of Father McNamy's burial day, word ran through the novitiate that the Sox had won the pennant. Brother McCarthy had brought the news straight from Father Master's office, to which, it was discreetly whispered, Brothers Lavelle and Corning had been summoned. But the biggest news was Brother McCarthy's permission.

Despite his known aversion to anything academic, Father Master had asked Brother McCarthy if he wanted to study the New Testament in Greek for fifteen minutes every day. Brother McCarthy had much to say about the shortage of scholars and the importance of getting at the real meaning of the New Testament, none of which impressed his listeners so much as the bare fact that he had obviously been chosen for an important position in the order. The more wary novices remained silent, the less wore their dismay upon their brows, but none was noticed by Brother Mc-Carthy, who alternated between joy at his confirmation in favor and worry that perhaps he had said too much about Brother Corning. Joy predominated, however.

His grief of the past two days had been, after all, grief over an absence. Now that absence was filled, and there lay before him clear, attainable goals and a personal fulfillment combining wisdom and piety in the service of God. Thus it was that his innocence was buried even before Father McNamy was in the ground.

On one of his many trips past Father Master's door, he could not help seeing Brother Lavelle come out and stand in the corridor, stunned.

"Is Father Master busy?" he asked. "I want to see him about where to put the guests after the funeral."

"He thinks I should leave." Brother Lavelle was white.

"Leave? You mean leave the Thomasites?" Brother McCarthy felt panic; he certainly hadn't meant to get them in that much trouble.

"Yes, leave." He stood there for a moment, began to scratch his ear, and stopped. "It's up to me, he says."

"Those aren't things we're supposed to tell each other, Brother. Father Master never wants anyone to know that somebody's leaving until he's left."

"Yes, well. I mean. Yes." And he went to chapel, where for an hour he cried as he had not cried in many years and as he never would again.

Father Master had not, in fact, told Brother Lavelle he should leave. He had with facility and tact congratulated Brother Lavelle on his progress in the religious life, had reminded him of the religious ideals proposed by the Thomasites, had gradually worked around to the lifestyle and the intellectual acumen necessary to his vocation.

He mentioned several illustrious Thomasites currently in the news, cited the brilliance of mind of Brothers even now in the novitiate—Brother McCarthy and Brother Corning, for instance

—and filled in details on a description of the order which, if not absolutely accurate, was undeniably impressive.

Finally he introduced the dreaded words: it might be well if Brother considered whether or not the Holy Spirit was really calling him to the Thomasites. What the Church needed today more than ever was dedicated laymen who listened to the teaching Church and who lived the spirit of Christ in a world that had forgotten Him. The decision was of course up to himself, but there had been signs, small ones but strong, that indicated it would be best for Brother Lavelle to serve God as a layman.

None of this was lost on Brother Lavelle, who quite accurately translated the talk into "He thinks I should leave." It was a full two days before he realized Father Master was right, a week before he left the Thomasites forever.

Brother McCarthy was standing at the door when Brother Corning appeared for his interview.

"*Morituri, te salutamus.*" He flashed Brother McCarthy the smile that would one day decorate *Time* magazine, but Brother McCarthy was not to be taken in.

"I'm not in a rush, Brother. You can go ahead of me," he said, sitting down on the bench opposite Father Master's door in a way that told Brother Corning he would find him there when he finally came out, shamefaced.

"You're very kind, Brother McCarthy." And then, just as he knocked, he added, "You're a very kind bag of shit." He had no doubt as to the reason for his summons.

Father Master waved him to the seat beside his desk, a rocking chair in which it was impossible to feel comfort or dignity, a device Father had discovered many years ago for keeping novices in the proper frame of mind while he talked to them.

"How are you getting on in the novitiate, Brother Corning?" He sat back and slowly, aimlessly, shuffled through the papers before him, papers that Brother Corning accurately guessed were from the file kept on him.

"Very well, thank you, Father. Except, I guess you know, I don't like baseball very much." Let's get at it, Brother Corning thought.

"I see. I see." Father Master belched softly. He was often that way mornings, a surprising weakness in a man so self-controlled, some novices said; others said he did it deliberately to suffer the humiliation. He belched again, this time not so softly. "Excuse me, Brother."

Brother Corning toyed with the chair and said nothing.

"So you don't like baseball very much, you say. Well, Brother. We've come here to suffer and die for Christ, not to have a good time for Him. That's what St. Teresa said, and I agree with her. Baseball isn't the most important thing in the life of a Thomasite, eh?"

"Yes, Father." And he laughed.

"You're laughing, Brother. You do a lot of laughing." Father Master's statement was noncommittal. There was no response. "Well, Brother, that's fine. That's fine. There are a few things, though, that I want to talk to you about." He leaned back in his chair and, folding his hands on his stomach, belched softly toward heaven.

"Yes, Father."

"A few things, Brother. First of all, there is the matter of your language. We've spoken of that before, and I think we need say no more, except to tell you that these words must be eliminated from your vocabulary."

Brother Corning, thinking many things, thought it better to say nothing.

"Is that clear?" His tone was suddenly dictatorial.

"Yes, Father, that's clear. I'm sorry about what I called Brother McCarthy."

"I did not mention Brother McCarthy or any of your Brothers. This is not the point, Brother Corning. The point is that your language is offensive and it must be removed."

Brother Corning bowed his head penitently, trying to think of what the *it* could possibly refer to.

"Now, as for some other things."

Second of all, Brother Corning thought, and unconsciously wagged his head in imitation of Brother McCarthy.

"Second of all, there is a severe violation of the rules reported recently. Violation of *numquam duo*; violation of *numquam duo during* the baseball game. It is reported that you went off alone with a certain one of your Brothers and, what is worse, that you were alone with him while you were supposed to be at another duty. Exclusivity, Brother Corning, is a very serious offense."

Father Master paused to let the seriousness of the offense impress Brother Corning, who merely sat there, not rocking exactly, but toying with the chair in the most aggravating way.

"Well, Brother, why did you do it?"

"Brother Lavelle and I are friends."

"Did you say friends? Did you say Brother Lavelle and you are friends?" He spoke less in anger than in disbelief. No good novice ever had friends.

"Yes, Father." Perhaps, he thought, I've gone too far. "Yes, we're friends. We went swimming and we had a good talk about . . ."

"Friends! Brother Corning, you are a novice. It is my duty to explain to you once and for all that friendship is a great and wonderful thing. Friendship is fine for adults. But I assure you, Brother Corning, friendship will happen in my novitiate only over my dead body!" His voice had built to a dramatic crescendo. "Do you, Brother Corning, understand me, what I am saying to you?"

"Yes, Father, I understand you." He paused, then added in a tone of genuine contrition, "Brother Lavelle and I will stop being friends. Nor shall I make any other friends. I understand, Father." You creepy bastard, he thought.

"And third of all, Brother." Father Master suddenly breathed heavily. He was not accustomed to displaying anger, and his accelerated pulse alarmed him. "Third of all, and this is embarrassing for both of us, I must inform you of your feminine traits."

Brother Corning had met many homosexual painters passing through his father's studio; surely Father Master could not be about to accuse him of this also.

"Feminine traits, Father?"

"I'm sorry to say it, Brother. Not the fact that you don't like baseball, although I do think you might ask yourself why. No, it's something more than that. First of all, there is your painting. That is a feminine occupation, a feminine thing, Brother. Now I know there's an excuse; your mother paints, or is it your father—well, no matter. It's only one thing. Second of all, you work with Brother

O'Callahan on the flowers instead of on the farm. Flowers, Brother!"

"But I was assigned . . ."

"Never interrupt when I'm talking, Brother. That is insolent. Do you understand?"

"Yes, Father. I beg your pardon."

"Third of all, your association with Brother Lavelle. It is exclusive, and exclusivity always militates against charity and against the rule. It is a very dangerous thing, and I think you will find, Brother, that this relationship finds its roots in your feminine traits."

There was a long pause. Brother Corning felt sure he could hear Brother McCarthy smiling outside the door. He began to blush, which convinced Father Master he had made his point. He sat back, relieved. These problems were always the most difficult.

"All right now, Brother, what are we going to do about this?"

"Well, Father," he lied, "I shall be careful of these things. I shall be careful to form no more friendships." That should get him, he thought. May he fry in hell.

"I had something more definite in mind, Brother." He waited. "Can you guess what that is?"

Castration? And aloud he said, "No, I can't, Father."

"I was thinking, Brother, that perhaps the Holy Spirit has something different for you in mind. I was thinking that perhaps you'd be happier as a layman." Brother Corning registered no response whatsoever. "Of course, it's your decision, Brother."

You're Goddamned right it's my decision, he thought. For the second time in his life, Brother Corning wanted desperately to be a priest. He made thinking a defense; his face betrayed nothing.

"I have no more to say, Brother, except that you must think and pray about this. When you have reached your decision, you will see me. Of course, in the meanwhile I shall be thinking and praying about it also. The Spirit is always with us when we humbly open ourselves to Him, Brother. The Holy Spirit will teach us all truth, a great Thomasite saying."

"If that's all, Father, I'd like to go and pray about this now."

"Prayer, prayer is the answer, Brother. Prayer and mortification. Oh, and Brother, until you've made your decision to leave—or to stay, of course—there will be no further ideas about painting or about making friends. Is that clear?"

"That's clear." I'll be a priest. I'll be a Thomasite priest and a first-rate painter despite you, he thought, and furthermore I'll dedicate my first show to you: *To my Master of Novices, without whom these paintings would never have been possible*. He did this nine years later at a time when the irony was lost on Father Master, though not on Richard Lavelle. "That's clear, Father. No painting. No friends. No flowers, either, I suppose?"

"No flowers, Brother."

"No flowers. Yes, Father, that's very clear. And I promise you I'll do better."

"That's fine, Brother. That's fine." He dismissed him with a vague feeling of apprehension. There was something subtly dishonest about Brother Corning. Yet one must never judge the interior.

Brother Corning went directly to chapel, where he waited until Brother Lavelle came out. Brother Lavelle would not hear of skipping the funeral, nor did they speak again until two days had passed and Brother Lavelle's decision had been made. The next five days they were together as often as possible, though keeping out of sight of the enemy occupied the greater part of their time.

* * *

A good day. A very good day. Father Master sighed with the contentment of a man who has undertaken many difficult jobs and has done them all well. It was very late, ten-thirty, and all the invited priests had retired to rooms to finish drinking Father McNamy's health or, when they remembered, his eternal beatitude.

The day had been busy but good. Breakfast was fine. Then the conference on Father McNamy, appropriate on the day of his funeral, even if it wasn't altogether true. But it could have been true, and should have, if only Father McNamy had looked on the positive side of things. Well, a little emphasis on virtue never hurt a story. A good conference.

Brother McCarthy, fine lad, had been very grateful, properly grateful, for his privilege. God knows, there was no choice about giving it once Major Superiors wrote saying pick three men and start them. It was enough, at the beginning, to start with one.

Then Brother Lavelle. He would be out in less than a week. A boy responsive to the Spirit, but hopelessly unsuited for religious life.

Brother Corning was a special problem. Would he leave? Impossible to say. Well, God forbid that we should ever be responsible for losing a true vocation. The Spirit would have His way. We shall not interfere. Though he doesn't belong; that friendship business was a sure sign.

Then the funeral. A lovely funeral. It was a sad thing, to be sure, that fewer priests showed up for the funeral than had planned on coming to the jubilee. Food left over. Still, it was nice to meet old friends. Sports holiday. A drink before dinner. Father O'Toole, blessedly, had taken sick before they went into dinner so that none of the novices were witness to the spectacle. A terrible disease, alcohol. Some fine men ruined by it. Then dinner and the conversation afterward, not always religiously becoming. A good cigar. A small brandy, for company's sake. And now the lake with the moon on it, a more slender ribbon, a more narrow path, but gleaming there still like a pathway to heaven.

The Sox had won the pennant. The impossible dream. Just so in the spiritual life. The impossible dream is sometimes realized. Father Master knelt in thanksgiving for a good day and a good life. Tomorrow's conference must return to the rules, the one on the proper manner of holding the dress. An unfortunate rule, as difficult to talk about as wrinkles on the nose.

A FEW NECESSARY QUESTIONS

"Your name?"

"Paul Gregoire."

"Address?"

"I, well, I'm staying at a hotel until I can find a place . . . a flat."

"Phone number?"

"I don't know. Oh, here it is: 373-2455. But . . ."

"I have what I need, then, Mr. Gregory. But we cannot be of help to you over the phone, Mr. Gregory, unless you come into the office. We only do business in the office."

"Yes, of course."

"All right, then. Cheerio."

She hung up. Paul Gregoire looked into the dead phone for a minute—he hadn't thought people actually said "cheerio"—and then he also hung up. He had spent four days walking through Kensington and Chelsea looking for a flat, and of course he had found nothing. The hotel clerk, who was anxious to be rid of him, suggested he try an agency, Wasps or London Flats. He did, and now he hung up the phone and once again began to cry.

He cried almost soundlessly—the hotel walls were so thin—and rocked back and forth hugging his knees. He was crying because he had learned only recently that you are either living or dead, and he knew he had a choice to make. In less than an hour he stopped crying and walked down the corridor to the bathroom, where he threw up again and again. He washed and went off to London Flats on Gloucester Road.

* * *

Pudding, someone said.

Paul Gregoire studied the stitching on his shoe and tried not to frame a response.

Bread pudding.

Chocolate pudding.

Rice pudding.

Plum pudding, but that was something different, a cake.

Figgy pudding. Somewhere crippled children were singing, "we all love a figgy pudding," stridently, relentlessly. How could they do this, make themselves a parody of happiness, a Christmas joke? He wanted them to stop. It was cruel, it was unspeakable, to allow innocence to mock itself this way. He wanted to hit them, to twist their stunted arms and make them stop. "We all love a figgy pu-u-dding." A child reached out to him. He snatched the arm and twisted it hard, but it was so thin and fragile in his grip that he grew frightened and dropped it. His fingerprints were seared into the flesh. The child looked up at him, waiting for whatever would come next. "So bring some right now."

He rested, leaning against the wall that surrounds the Brompton Oratory. And then he slammed his right hand against the stones until it was puffy and blood ran freely from the broken flesh of the knuckles.

* * *

That night at the hotel he wrote on the back of a paper bag. "London Flats on Gloucester Road is a long dark closet with three desks, each overseen by an angry young woman. The first looks like Princess Anne but with even less chin; the second never appears except in a black silk dress—her name is Elise and from the way the others refer problems to her she appears to have seniority or at least dispository rights over the more attractive apartments; the third is milk white and fluffy blond, as if she were composed of mashed potatoes with chicken gravy. We sit on a bench along the wall: teen-age boys with hair to their shoulders; blushing young secretaries who want a bed sitter for five pounds a week; widows on pension hoping for a single room with a heating coil; four or five Indians (there are Indians everywhere in London; every occupied phone booth contains at least one Indian); two sleek homosexuals looking for a convenient *pied-à-terre*; and I, Paul Gregoire, American, ex-priest, waiting, studying the stitching on my shoe."

He folded the bag so that "Boots the Chemist" faced up, and then he slipped it between his shirts in the bureau drawer, where the cleaning woman found it the next morning on her appointed rounds.

* * *

"And so you entered to save your soul."

"Yes, Father."

"And the souls of others."

"Yes."

"In short, to save the world."

"Father, I never had such . . ."

"Yes or no."

"I can't say."

"You must say. These things have to be simplified. Matters of the soul are complex beyond all human understanding, and the particular distinctions that one priest wants to make in discussing the nature of his vocation and his fall from it have to be reduced to the realizable, the comprehensible. Rome is patient, but you must answer. Now, yes or no."

"Yes."

"So you entered to save the world and found yourself pitying it." The old priest waited. "That *is* what your story seemed to imply."

"Yes. I don't know. Yes."

"And then fearing it."

"Yes."

"You feared what you came to save."

"Yes, but I don't mean pity the way it comes out when you say whatever you said, and what I fear isn't something frightening, it's the stark madness of good people doing evil and not knowing, it's . . ."

"My son, my good man, you are not on trial. We imply no value judgments here. The facts are all we want. You desire to leave the priesthood, and I am here to examine your case. Only facts. Now we will go back. You entered to save your soul."

* * *

"Fr. McDonnell's room is a coffin stood on end," Paul Gregoire wrote. "I began to sweat and then to shake. I don't think he realized I was crying." He drew a line beneath this and wrote, "Was there not even one priest at Dachau?" And then another line and, "I must stop listening to what is not being said."

Reading this the next morning, the cleaning woman concluded that he was indeed strange, even for an American.

* * *

Elise Smythe had dismissed the Indians and, lighting another cigarette, fumbled through her packet of soiled cards, muttering quietly and puffing. "Next," she called without bothering to look up. "Next, please, next."

Paul Gregoire approached her desk and sat down on a very old kitchen chair, which at once gave way beneath him.

Elise looked up sharply and frowned. "Careful," she said, "the leg isn't on proper." And frowning still, she reached into her dress and gave a firm tug to a strap. Then with a little arch of her back, she slung her breasts across the desk as if she expected him to do something with them or at least comment on them. It was, he would discover, merely her way, part of a separate performance played out for each customer. It had nothing to do with anything.

"Name."

"Paul Gregoire."

She inhaled deeply and leaned back, studying his suit, his tie, his coarse American accent. He could afford sixteen pounds at least.

"You're looking for what, then, Mr. Gregory?"

"Well, actually, what I'd like is a place with one bedroom, perhaps in Kensington."

"How much?"

"I thought perhaps twelve or fifteen pounds a week."

"Impossible," she said, "out of the question."

"I see. Well, what do they rent for?"

She hadn't heard. She was not going to hear.

"Around here?" she said, "twelve or fifteen pounds a week around *here?*" She waved her hand grandly, and he realized that with that gesture she had made the Underground station across the street, the Wimpy Bar next door, the unspeakably shabby office in which they sat—she had made all of them disappear and they were, Paul Gregoire and Elise Smythe, at tea in Kensington Gardens. He sat silent while she looked at her scene for a moment more and then, abruptly, she descended. In an almost chummy manner she said, "You've got to go up to sixteen. Fifteen won't ever do it. Never. Sixteen is good; and eighteen. But don't go over eighteen. It's not worth it, not around here."

* * *

"Are you or are you not?"

"But what? I don't know what you want to know."

"Are you or are you not a Jew."

"But I'm a Catholic priest. You know that. Of course I'm not a Jew."

"We thought you'd say that."

"I'm not."

"Why do you keep protesting? Do you hate the Jews?"

"No; if anything, I like them."

"'Some of my best friends are Jews,' is that what you're saying? Why do you condescend to them? Is it a coverup?"

"I *am* a Jew." He was shouting; he could hear his voice rising, strong above the other noises. They were getting a needle ready, preparing the injection. Two of them wrestled him to the floor, and another tore off his trousers. "I *am*, I *am* a Jew," he shouted, although he knew he was not.

He felt the sharp jab of the needle in his left buttock, and then someone turned him over on his back.

"Now we can go to work on him," a voice said.

* * *

For over an hour he cried soundlessly, hugging his knees, rocking back and forth. And for another hour he stared at the Boots bag. Then he wrote.

"Elise Smythe is a hastily assembled mobile of fruits and vegetables. Her mouth is a badly puckered crabapple, her breasts are canteloupes. And when she walks, her buttocks resemble two oddly shaped watermelons." He paused for a moment and then continued. "She is hanging on the way you grip the window ledge in nightmares just before you wake up." There was no more room to write.

The cleaning woman took the shirts out of their plastic containers. They were new shirts, neither had yet been worn, and she removed the pins with elaborate care. Unfolding the shirts on the bed, she admired the material for a moment, caressing it between her thumb and forefinger, and then, with a quick glance over her shoulder, she slit the two shirts from the hem of the tail to the little collar button in back. She folded them, replacing the pins and the cardboard stiffener exactly as they had been, and then she put them back in the bureau drawer, the Boots bag just as she had found it.

* * *

At half past ten in the morning Mrs. Rivers had already had her elevenses: gin and a piece of toast. She leaned against the doorway, one hand on her hip, one at her throat. She blinked into the sunlight and tried to focus.

"Miss Smythe sent me," he said. "From London Flats."

"You're Mr. Gregory?"

"Paul Gregoire, actually. It's a French name."

"Gregoire. You're younger than I expected. I expected someone not so young. She said on the phone that you write for *Life* magazine. I thought you'd be older."

Paul Gregoire had once ghostwritten a review of a theological book and, although *Life* paid for it, they had never printed it. Pressed by Elise Smythe for his present (none) and then his previous occupations (also none), he lamely admitted that he had once done a review for *Life*.

"I'm thirty-three. It was only a review, actually."

"Well, if you work for *Life*, you must know me."

"Oh, are you connected with *Life*?"

"*You* ought to know, if you work for *Life*. *Life* did a perfectly enormous story about us. The Riverses. The last of the White Rajahs. That's what this is." She jabbed him with her pointed fingers, on one of which glittered a very large diamond. "That's a reward for twenty-five years of living with wogs."

"Wogs?"

"Oh Christ, *Africa!* We were the last of the White Rajahs."

"I see."

"Look, do you want to see the flat or don't you?"

She pushed ahead of him, and with surprising agility led him down a narrow flight of outdoor stairs. They descended in a heavy mist of gin and perfume.

She was talking, endlessly talking. Paul Gregoire looked at the wiry hair, the deep furrows in her brow, her cheeks caked with powder that had begun to crack. Her lashes were heavy with mascara, and in the corner of one of her dim gray eyes, pus had gathered. She was seventy, he thought, and pickled in alcohol. She was talking about the previous occupant, a French girl—from France—who had a lover, and what a mess they had left the flat.

He was not listening, and he was only faintly aware of the apartment; it was small and cold and filthy, a likely tomb for the last of the White Rajahs.

"Well?" she said.

"I'm sorry, what was that?"

"I said eighteen pounds a week, take it or leave it."

"Eighteen pounds." Ridiculous, it wasn't worth ten. "Eighteen pounds," he said, "that sounds all right."

Paul Gregoire could not look at her as she kneaded his shoulder, as the tightened planes of her face cracked in a smile. He had handed her salvation with a lie. Again, as always, it had been so easy.

* * *

He had a new Boots bag, a smaller one; it had contained tranquilizers. He smoothed it out tenderly.

"Pity and even compassion can destroy. Empty hearts do not count; we have always had them. Only the full ones matter."

He rose then and, for no reason other than that he did these things, he went to the bureau and took out his new shirts. Rapidly he tore away the plastic bags, the pins, the cardboard. The shirts were ruined.

Later he wrote simply, "Do you see?"

* * *

"Now, Mr. Gregory, you are an American?"

"Gregoire, Father. Yes, American."

"I see. Well, how does it happen that you have come to England to apply for laicization? You ought to have done this in America. The paperwork is horrific." He belched and patted his paunch by way of apology. Pouring himself a glass of wine, he said, "For my stomach, you know. Paul recommended it to Timothy, unless I'm mistaken."

"About the papers, Father. I came to England. *Then* I decided."

"So much the worse. You know, of course, that Father McDonnell has sent you to see me, because your testimony was not satisfactory. Whereas he finds no fault in you, he sees no grounds on which you might be granted a decree of laicization. You have been, it seems, an adequate priest, if a bit overly zealous. Seems you are unwilling to accept your human limitations. He says you cry."

Paul Gregoire, holding back tears, said nothing.

"Very well, to begin. Your name?"

* * *

"Poor John."

"Poor Elspeth, you mean."

They left then, two elderly ladies, beautifully dressed, who had spent the evening sipping vintage port at Yates Wine Lodge in the Strand. Paul Gregoire, who had been eavesdropping, paid for his sherry and followed them. They were old and they were giddy, so he had to pace himself carefully, dallying behind them and then catching up and passing. Take out the Underground map, examine it until they catch up, let them pass, and then follow once more. He had been doing this sort of thing for weeks now. It was the only contact he chose to have with the living.

"But poor John, with that nose."

"What about the nose?"

"My dear, it's so big and long."

"John has a long nose, and flat, like a duck's bill."

"Exactly it, long and flat like a duck's bill."

They stopped to laugh and to hold each other up. Paul Gregoire passed them. In a minute he would stop to study his map.

"And his eyes. Poor John. Some men have nice eyes and that makes up, but not John."

"Not John. John has shockin' eyes."

"John has shockin' eyes and a nose like a duck's bill. Poor John."

Two drunken old ladies, laughing and laughing, and here am I, he thought, what?

"John has shockin' eyes," he wrote on a laundry ticket and put it back into his wallet. He smiled.

*   *   *

"You mustn't be discouraged, Mr. Gregory, it's very hard to find a place in London." Elise Smythe pulled hard on her cigarette and sent a steady stream of smoke into his eyes.

"Perhaps something more expensive. I'd be willing to pay more for something I really wanted."

"Very wise, Mr. Gregory." She nodded approval of his wisdom. "You often have to pay an awful lot to get what you really want."

* * *

Dear Father Gregoire: I have been in A.A. now for over a year and I want you to know that I owe it all to you. I could never of done it without you. To me you are a Saint of God and I mention you every meeting at the A.A. You have brought me back to life. Thank you very much. Sincerely, Ralph B. Otter.

Paul Gregoire stood on Waterloo Bridge turning the letter over and over in his hands. After a long time, a very long time, he came to a decision, and it was the letter that fluttered from the rail to the dark waters beneath.

* * *

"Guilty or not guilty?"
"Guilty."
"Elise?"
"Smythe."
"Tears?"
"None."
"Pudding?"
"Pudding?"
"Again: pudding?"
"Oh, yes. Figgy."
"Pity?"
"Murder."
"Yes or no?"
"I can't . . ."
"Yes or no?"
"Yes."

* * *

" 'The waste remains, the waste remains and kills'—Empson." He wrote on the flap of his airplane ticket.

* * *

"Your name?"

"Paul Gregoire."

"This your passport?"

"Yes."

The customs inspector called a police officer. "He says this is his passport." They both studied the photo and then the man. The policeman shrugged.

"Nothing to declare?"

"No."

"Nothing?"

"Nothing."

"Open that."

Paul Gregoire opened the suitcase, and the customs official rooted among the tee shirts, the socks, the soiled evidence of three years in England.

"What's this?"

"Those are tranquilizers. I don't use them any longer."

"Well, well, well." The customs inspector whistled. "We'll just hold onto these if you don't mind."

"I don't use them any more. It doesn't matter."

"What's this thing?"

"It's a case for my contact lenses."

He whistled again, studied the little plastic vial with care, and placed it apart with the tranquilizers. After half an hour everything in the suitcase had been examined, and a neat pile of evidence lay to one side.

"Step behind that screen."

Behind the screen three men watched while Paul Gregoire removed his clothing. They picked up each item, pulled at the seams of his shirt, felt his trouser cuffs. They made him stoop over, made him raise his arms. Finally they had checked everything, looked into his mouth, searched beneath his arms, spread his legs, and examined his crotch. They had found nothing.

Sweating with frustration, furious, one of them punched him lightly but repeatedly in the ribs. "Okay," he said, "okay, what are you hiding?"

"Nothing," Paul Gregoire said, naked but suddenly invulnerable.

The punch came harder. "Open up, you bastard, what are you hiding?"

There was a long silence while the man raised his fist and then dropped it again.

"God." He said it simply, as if it were true. He did not smile.

They let him go then, realizing he wasn't dangerous after all, just another nut.